MICHAEL BOULERICE

FEEDING THE WHEEL

DEATH'S HEAD PRESS

T0407902

Published by Death's Head Press,

an imprint of Dead Sky Publishing, LLC

Miami Beach, Florida

www.deadskypublishing.com

Cover by Luke Spooner

Design & Formatting by Apparatus Revolution, LLC

Edited by Anna Kubik and Megan Yundt

Copyedited by Vivian Wong

To Alex Woodroe,

My dear friend, editor, soothsayer, and wolf kin.

You're getting your entire ass kicked at darts the next time I see you.

CHAPTER
ONE

I sat alone in my home office; a teabag filled with self-loathing and remorse steeping in the remains of my once exceptional life. Stock tickers and financial projections flashed on a monitor I no longer had any interest in. I stared at a stack of bills to my left. I chuckled grimly as I realized, regardless of how tonight's events would unfold, I'd likely never have to worry about paying them.

Dusk was turning to night outside my window. There wasn't much time left to sit and feel sorry for myself. I'd have to meet the Children soon. Head deep into the woods. Finish what we started all those years ago. Stop the cycle we'd been caught in for over thirty years. Make it right.

Or die trying. That was the only other acceptable option.

My temples throbbed from the concussive blows of a tension headache as I sat there, my mind drifting as it often did to the first time we fed the Wheel. The house was empty of voices and footsteps, freeing it to speak in the creaks and ticks that scared me as a child in my darkened bedroom that is now, or was, my eldest daughter's.

The bedroom that served as a stage for the beginning of it all.

It had been a BB pinging off glass that roused me from my spaceman sheets the night before the first day of seventh grade. Marley, my best friend from across the street, and I originally used pebbles, because actors used them in movies to wake each other up without their parents noticing, but I'd cracked Marley's window the third time we'd tried it, so we switched over to the carton of BBs we used as ammo for my slingshot. They were just as loud without the risk of breaking anything.

I slid my window open, pausing briefly to lament my lanky pre-teen frame and latest crop of acne in the reflection, and squinted into the backyard. Marley stood there, greasy hair and freckled face bathed in moonlight, poised to throw a brick through my window if I hadn't answered. It was the last night we'd be able to sneak out before the first day of school, and he wanted to make sure it was the best and longest adventure yet. He offered me our practiced hand sign that signaled the coast was clear. I slid my sneakers on and climbed outside to meet him.

Marley whispered at me like a hissing snake. "Caleb, you idiot. You fell asleep again, didn't you? I told you to stay awake and wait for me."

"I couldn't help it." I stage whispered back. "Mom gave me Benadryl for my poison ivy. It makes me sleepy."

Out of pure boredom, we'd started sneaking out of our houses in search of excitement that summer. We explored our quiet little cul-de-sac by the light of the moon, as flashlights could give us away that early in the morning. We rifled through our neighbors' station wagons and picked through newly built garages that still smelled like fresh lumber, just to see what kind of stuff they had.

There were only twelve houses in the development, ten if you took ours away, so we inevitably ran out of things to investigate. That was when we took to the woods.

Our houses were surrounded by protected woodlands. It was a miracle the developer was able to carve out a little piece of it for us. That was what the dads would say to each other at neighborhood barbecues as they drank cold cans of beer and traded lawn care secrets. A stretch of road coursed along the western edge of the conservation area, but everything to the east, north, and south of us was nothing but miles of ancient pines and scrub brush. As kids, we were pretty sure those woods stretched to infinity. Our parents allowed us to dip into the trees bordering our backyards, but never so far that we couldn't see our houses through the ever-thickening branches. And never at night.

For our woodland excursions, we broke protocol and brought flashlights with us. Moonlight couldn't penetrate that thick canopy, save for the occasional silver javelin bursting through to the forest floor like stage spotlights. We'd enter the woods at the end of the street, where it circled back on itself as a turnaround, to keep anyone from hearing our shoes crunching on the thick leaf crust of the forest floor. Once we were in deep enough, we clicked our flashlights on and explored the forbidden expanse together.

"Which way should we go?" I asked. Marley paid no attention to me, busying himself by adding newly discovered details to a gridded makeshift map as he walked. It was something he often did; beg me to hang out, only to ignore me in favor of something else. A video game. A bag of potato chips. A secret map of the woodlands he kept stashed underneath his mattress so his parents wouldn't find it. Like our time together was never enough for him.

"Hello? Earth to asshole? Do you read me?"

"What the hell do you want? Why are you always so needy?"

"I'm not needy. I'm asking which way you think we should go."

"Whatever, Baby Caby. Let's go this way." Marley pointed in the general direction of a patch of woods. Pissed about his attitude, I stomped ahead of him, forcing him to follow me instead.

We spent a couple hours zigging this way and that, scrambling over mossy rocks and through pucker brush, Marley complaining behind me as I forged ahead to what I was starting to think looked like a clearing. Marley didn't believe me at first. We hadn't found a break in the canopy once in all of our travels, but he could see the leaves above us giving way to a night sky positively riddled with stars as we got closer.

And then we found ourselves at the foot of a stony hill bathed in electric blue moonlight, staring up at that impossible Wheel.

It instantly reminded me of those old millstones you find repurposed as half-buried landscaping features in office parks and upscale condos as some kind of half-assed attempt to honor the local history they'd just eradicated. It was upright, made of what looked like regular old New Hampshire granite, and had a circular hole in the middle.

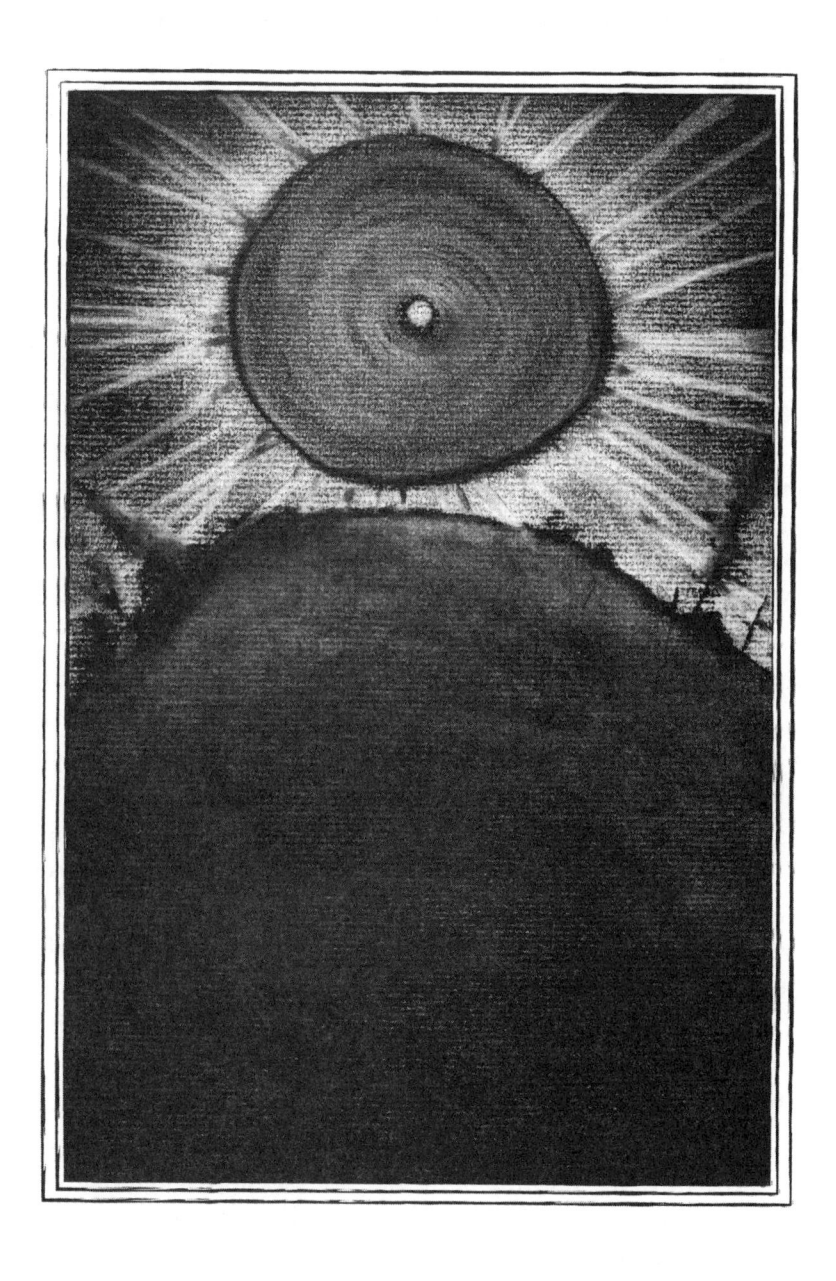

Only this millstone stretched as high as our two-story house. And it hovered a few inches above the ground without anything seeming to prop it up.

I could tell Marley had noticed that detail at the same time, because he was looking directly to either side of the enormous stone wheel, searching for some kind of guywires or super industrial fishing line; anything logical that could explain how a multi-ton stone disk could stay suspended in the air like that.

My brain screamed to rationalize what we were seeing. *We'd stumbled so far through the woodlands that we'd reached a different neighborhood. It was a party; a party rich people threw for their kids in their backyard. We were looking at a Ferris wheel they'd rented, that's all.* But it didn't stick. The feeling of wrongness about the scene made it impossible to lie to myself.

I was about to be the first one to break the silence, ready to verbalize the "what the fuck" that hung silently between us, when the singing began.

A melodic chorus of children's voices sounded from the top of the rocky hill. We couldn't see from our position at the bottom of it, but it was clear as day. It reminded me of the school concerts our music teacher was always forcing us to participate in, only in a language we couldn't understand. Marley and I looked at each other with terrified eyes as big as drink coasters. To this day, I can remember the feeling of panicked aloneness I'd experienced only once before that night, when I was very young, and my mother had accidentally lost me in a women's clothing store. It felt like someone had attached jumper cables to my heart. We knew without saying it that we'd finally gone too far, broken too many rules in the name of adventure. We'd been careless, and we'd found real danger because of it.

When we turned our gazes away from ourselves and back up at the Wheel, there was a young girl, maybe six or seven years old, staring back down at us from the top of the hill. She had brown hair that went past her shoulders, and wore what looked like an old-fashioned white nightgown. She had no shoes on. Looking at her somehow made me relax. It didn't make my fear and sense of wrongness disappear entirely, but it subdued them enough to make them less overwhelming.

I grabbed Marley's shoulder, signaling for us to retreat the way we'd come. He shrugged me off, and began scrambling up the rocky hill.

What are you doing?! I mouthed.

They're just kids, dude. Chill. He mouthed back.

I reached the top of the hill, and despite the strange children and giant floating Wheel—and it *was* floating—I couldn't pry my eyes away from the night sky above us. Those purplish pink gaseous nebulas that moved as I stared at them, the stars that were green and orange, and somehow meandering through deep space as defined shapes; definitely not the stars I looked at from my backyard. The moon was so big. How was it so big? There were other moons, too. Some with impossibly fast orbits that reminded me of basketballs spinning on the floor of a gym, and some which had fractured to pieces, yet somehow still formed the vague shapes of planets. I was so transfixed I didn't even hear Marley approach me. He was just standing next to me all of a sudden, marveling at the bright, wrong sky along with me.

A small, cool hand grabbed my own, jolting me out of my rapture. It was the young girl with the brown hair, who smiled up at me so serenely I could do nothing but smile back. *These kids are good people,* I thought as she led me closer to the Wheel, which seemed to emit a low, droning buzz.

A group of children, ages ranging from maybe six to ten, all wearing the same white nightgowns, formed a circle around the floating, humming Wheel. Each of them tightly clutched their hands together, giving the bizarre scene the affectation of prayer, or ritual. They sang that unearthly melody, which seemed to repeat the longer I listened. Although the words of the song were foreign to my ears, the tone of it seemed to calm my mind, and made my muscles, tired from all the hiking, feel rejuvenated. My protests to escape suddenly ceased, and an exceedingly rare look of serenity washed over Marley's perpetually pinched face.

Before we even knew it was happening, Marley joined the circle of children, clasping his hands together as they did, and began singing their song with them. Ashamed Marley would think I was a loser if I hung back, I did the same.

It didn't take me long to realize the strange words we were singing had somehow translated into English in our minds.

Praises due to Demelae!
Mother of Life and Strength
Blessing us with Her divine implement
We thrive not without offering
The Children of the Wheel nourish Demelae
In Her realm away from realms
Place away from places
Space away from spaces
We satiate Demelae until Her return!

The hum of the Wheel grew stronger as we sang the song over and over, the feeling of well-being and power building, coursing through us like an electrical current made of love and goodness.

Something rustled at the base of the hill, drawing Marley and I out of our trances. It was loud enough for the other children to hear, but they paid it no attention. Their singing only grew louder as we watched the thick pucker brush part, and something slender and not of this world made its way up the hill with horrifyingly long strides. It was fashioned from bittersweet vines and yellowing old animal bones. Its wooden joints groaned like branches in a high wind, and the dead leaves caught in its reedy ribcage rustled as it went. A grinning moose skull acted as a makeshift head that took in its surroundings with an air of casual superiority. A pair of chipmunks playfully scurried up and down its legs, unbothered by the unnatural being's presence. I felt hot urine soak my pajama pants, my feet glued to the grass beneath me. I was powerless to do anything but watch as the stilted humanoid creature closed the distance between us and itself.

Panicking, I turned to Marley. Tears streamed down his horror-stricken face, just unable to escape or even stop singing as I was as he took the monster in.

The Children of the Wheel continued their ritual as the monster made of woodland detritus summitted the rocky hill. Hunched over in the posture of a praying mantis, it still loomed over everyone, its head nearly reaching the hole at the center of the giant stone disk that hummed so loudly it made my eyes vibrate. It considered the children as they sang, their white-knuckled hands clamped tighter than ever, before bringing its thorny claws together and joining them in praise of their deity. The thing stood so close to us we could smell it, earthy leaf rot and the minty tang of splintered birch twigs. Its reedy howl coaxed terrified tears from me as we all stood around the floating stone Wheel.

And then, without warning, the monster gently picked up one of the children—the little girl who'd originally invited us up—and held her to its chest in a loving, almost fatherly embrace, which she returned. Flowers burst into bloom in patches across its nightmare body.

A hole, which was the only way I could describe what appeared roughly a hundred feet above the Wheel, materialized like a paper towel thrown on top of an ink spill. Twinkling stars slowly swirled around the edge of the hole, beyond which was nothing but perfect blackness standing against the multicolored swell of the night sky that was not *our* night sky.

The monster approached the thinnest edge of the humming disk, and outstretched its arms, effortlessly gripping the little girl's body so she faced the ground horizontally, and brought her still smiling face closer to the Wheel. Closer. Closer.

And then came the whirring buzz of something hard making contact with a knife sharpener, or a band saw. A streak of wet redness instantly circled the edge of the Wheel as the little girl's skull gave way.

It was then, in my horror and panic, that I understood why the floating stone Wheel was humming. It was so perfectly balanced that we couldn't even tell it was spinning, not even as close as we were. Not until we saw that poor girls head ground off to the neck. Gore clung to the underside of the Wheel as the monster fed the girl's convulsing body to the gigantic grinding Wheel, spraying off of it in a relentless rooster tail that shot directly into the swirling black hole above us all.

The spell of the song finally broken, Marley and I screamed, and frantically stumbled back down the hill, each of us losing our footing and rolling over sharp rocks and sapling pines until we reached the bottom. I remember checking to make sure I hadn't broken anything, and realizing the children had never stopped singing as their peer was murdered. I looked back once as the monster pressed the last bits of the little girl's feet into the Wheel, and then we sprinted in the general direction of home, not slowing our pace through the woodlands until we could see the clear-cut seam between the trees and the safety of our neighborhood.

CHAPTER
TWO

I remember lying in my bed and staring up at the ceiling the following morning, trying to make up my mind whether I'd simply dreamt the events of the night before, or if Marley and I actually experienced that scene deep in our forbidden woodlands. I finally got up after the third time Mom screamed about getting ready for the school bus.

"Good morning, Mr. Sleepy Head." Dad said as he pounded the dregs of his coffee cup and stood to kiss mom on his way out to the car. "Have a good first day of school, slugger!"

My mind was still transfixed on the events of the previous night. I watched my body dump a pair of Pop Tarts into the toaster, and open the fridge to grab the orange juice.

"Oh wow." Mom said as she assessed at me. "Looks like that Benadryl worked."

I looked down. The raw, red poison ivy rash covering both of my legs had completely disappeared overnight.

Later, as I was in the bathroom washing up before school, I saw the zits on my face had all but vanished as well. I was thrilled. One less thing for the big kids to bully me about.

I waited for the bus at the end of our street with the rest of the kids from the cul-de-sac, desperate to talk to Marley. He never arrived. I sat alone on that green vinyl bus seat in my new school clothes, sweating with panic that a monster might've plucked my best friend out of his bedroom window as he was sleeping, making him alone atone for our shared sin of intruding where we didn't belong. I felt crazy.

Marley finally showed his face in the third period social studies class with Mr. Richter we were both in, still holding his skateboard that a hallway monitor was inevitably going to tell him to store in his locker. He said his dad yelled at him for so long that morning that he'd missed the bus, and that his mom stopped for McDonald's breakfast as she dropped him off with an excuse note. I wanted to ask him what he remembered about the night before, but the bell rung, and Mr. Richter didn't approve of cross-chatter during class.

That sort of thing was always happening at Marley's house. His dad would hammer him about unimportant things, sometimes even joking about it to me in front of Marley as he bullied him over not having mowed perfect lines in the backyard, or told him he was useless because he didn't load the dishwasher just so. It made me uncomfortable. His mom was forever coddling him, but that wasn't good, either. She still cleaned his room, years after I'd been made to clean mine on my own. Sometimes Marley said he would purposefully avoid doing a chore, because the odds were high that his mom would break down and do it for her special little guy. His parents were polar opposites that, at least to my underdeveloped sense of how things were supposed to be for kids, seemed like they were playing tug of war with his brain. My mom and dad never took me seriously when I'd bring it up to them, because Marley's dad was charming at neighborhood parties, and he did so much volunteer work, and he made so much money, and his mom was just so sweet. "You're not exactly great at chores yourself, slugger." I'd assume my parents were right because they were adults, so I'd drop it.

"You have thirty minutes to finish, startiiiiiinng..." Mr. Richter glanced up at the clock on the wall, waiting for the ticking red second hand to reach the black twelve. "Now."

I hadn't even noticed the Xeroxed pop quiz that had been slid on top of my desk. My heart thrummed. I rifled through the pages, hoping I'd recognize something. *Anything.* The first half of the quiz was multiple-choice, which soothed me a bit because at least it gave me a chance to guess, but the ass end of those pages was all essay questions. I was done for, even if I magically managed to guess every single lettered question correctly, which was impossible. I looked over at Marley. The room was still muggy with early September humidity, but not so much to explain away the sweat glistening on his head and neck. He was struggling as much as I was. I remember randomly looking down at his left calf because he was wearing shorts, and wondering why I couldn't spot the pink little scar he got falling in the driveway while we were playing whiffle ball.

I turned back to my quiz. I couldn't just hand it in empty. I closed my eyes, and took a few deep breaths, attempting to summon whatever scraps of Great Depression and Industrial Revolution trivia knowledge I had hiding in the nooks and crannies of my young brain.

And then I started.

Marley and I commiserated with each other about starting seventh grade off with what would likely be Fs in the hallway after class. I asked him about the woods.

"I don't know. Maybe it was just a dream. Listen, I have to get to science. We'll talk later, OK?"

I wanted to ask how we possibly could have had the same dream, but he was already down the hall, lost in a sea of Jansport backpacks and Adidas Sambas.

The bell rang just as I skidded into the locker room. The other kids were already dressed in their gym clothes and filing onto the basketball court, so I had to scramble to get my shorts and t-shirt on.

I'd immediately assumed I'd jinxed myself by thinking the day couldn't possibly get any worse, because when I ran out to meet the rest of the class, I saw it was rope climb day. A thin navy-blue pad was situated under a thick white rope, the bane of my school years, that stretched all the way up to the rafters.

"Ah, Caleb. There you are. Almost marked you absent." The gym teacher, Ms. Banquard, checked my name off on her clipboard. "Congratulations, you get to go first."

I sighed in resignation, and gripped the coarse, splintery rope with clammy hands. The stares from the circle of students surrounding me felt like drills boring into my tortured soul. I wasn't going to get three feet off the ground before my gangly arms gave up like they always did, and they were going to laugh about it for weeks. Months, maybe.

"Ready when you are, Caleb." Ms. Banquard folded her arms across her chest, and impatiently tapped one impossibly white tennis shoe on the squeaky parquet floor.

I gulped, closed my eyes, and lifted myself up enough to partially lock the thick rope between my knees and feet. I kept my eyes crammed shut as I repeated those steps, trying hard to visualize myself rising higher and higher off the ground; so high I could run a sweaty finger through the clumpy dust I'd always imagined clung to those steel rafters.

"That's enough, Caleb! Jesus H. Christ, you ate your Wheaties this summer, didn't you."

I stopped, opened my eyes, and almost fainted. My head was inches away from the knotted end of the rope. I'd climbed maybe twenty-five feet past the red duct tape line that signaled how high you were supposed to go. I wasn't even winded. I looked down and saw everyone looking up at me, mouths gaping with shock.

"Alright, showboat. Come on down before you hurt yourself. I'll have to check, but I'm pretty sure that's a new school record."

Before I descended to high fives and congratulations, I dreamily ran one of my fingers through the dust of the rafters, leaving behind a mark to prove to myself that I'd actually made it that far.

CHAPTER
THREE

Marley and I finally caught back up with each other at lunch. We sat at a cafeteria table away from everyone else, and I told him about what happened in gym class.

Marley looked at me unbelievingly as he shoveled a forkful of nuclear orange colored mac and cheese into his mouth. "I've watched you climb that rope a thousand times, Caleb. You've *never* made it over my head."

"I know, dude! It's crazy! Maybe my muscles are finally coming in."

My best friend looked me up and down, appraising me. "Yeah. No."

"Listen, we need to talk about last—"

I was interrupted by the buzz and squawk of the intercom system speaker in the corner of the room.

WILL MARLEY CLANGFORD AND CALEB SMITH PLEASE REPORT TO THE PRINCIPAL'S OFFICE. MARLEY CLANGFORD AND CALEB SMITH. THANK YOU.

We looked at each other as a chorus of "Ooohs" and "They're in trouuuuuuuuubles" filled the cafeteria.

After a brief wait in the hallway, the school secretary opened a door for us, and Marley and I filed into Mr. Silby's office. Neither of us had ever been in the principal's office before. We gawked at the framed wildlife photos he must've taken on some African safari vacation, and at the framed photos of his family on his desk, which seemed just as exotic. At that age, the concept of the fearsome authorities in your life also having wives and children and homes is a little jarring.

Mr. Silby was sitting at his desk, and signaled for us to sit in the two chairs in front of it. We did. Mr. Richter, our social studies teacher, stood cross-armed near Mr. Silby, and he looked mad.

"Boys, do you know why I called you in here?"

"No, sir." Marley and I said in unison.

"Of course they know." Mr. Richter said, his hands shifting to his hips, leaning in so close to our faces we could smell the rancid coffee on his breath.

"Steven, please." Mr. Silby gave Mr. Richter a look that made him step back, but he stared at us as if we'd taken turns shitting in his coffee thermos. "Do either of you have anything to say about the quiz you took in Mr. Richter's class today?"

Marley and I looked at each other with doom on our faces. Had we failed so hard the principal had to be involved?

"I'm sorry, sir. We didn't read as much as we were supposed to this summer. We just guessed as best as we could. We promise to do better."

"Please don't tell my dad." Marley said, his lower lip quivering.

Mr. Richter barked out a humorless laugh that earned him a second, sterner look from Mr. Silby. The social studies teacher once folded his arms across his chest, and spun around to face the wall behind him as he collected himself.

"Kids, the reason you're in here is because you both received perfect marks on your quizzes. The only two hundreds out of the entire class, and, well...neither of you have ever demonstrated grades like—"

"You two boys are D students, C at best when I'm generous. You cheated. Admit it."

"Steven, out. Now. We'll talk later."

Mr. Richter snatched their quizzes from the principal's desk, and offered a huffy "This is ridiculous!" before storming out of the room.

"I'm sorry about that, boys. You see, he's frustrated because you two, well, you don't get grades like this often. I'm afraid I have to agree with Mr. Richter. You're both getting out-of-school suspensions for a week."

I remember staring down at my shoelaces, feeling as if the air had been punched out of my chest. Suspension? My parents were going to kill me. At the very least, I was staring down the barrel of being grounded for a month *on top* of the punishment from school, and Marley? His dad might have actually killed him. I could feel the tears coming, and I resented them more than anything in the world. *Tears in front of Marley.* I'd never live it down.

"We didn't cheat."

When those words left Marley's mouth, I wanted to die. I wanted my soul to levitate out of my body and float anywhere that wasn't Mr. Silby's office. I knew Marley was desperate because a suspension would make his life at home unbearable, but he could never just let something go. There was no dignified resignation in him at all. He always had to find some loophole in an impossible situation that got him what he wanted. Marley was successful enough with kids their own age, but adults? It always ended badly. Marley was about to double our suspension, and I was powerless to do anything but watch it happen.

Mr. Silby sighed and leaned back in his chair. "I'll be calling your parents shortly. Clean out your lockers. I don't need the janitor complaining about a rotten sandwich stinking up the hallway while you're gone."

"We didn't cheat."

"But you did, Marley. You'd be wise to cool your jets and just accept it."

Marley stood up, red-faced and shaking. I gulped.

"We didn't cheat."

Mr. Silby stood and jutted a furious finger at Marley. "You want to make that a two week suspension? Because I can accommodate."

I had a split second wonder if I was actually psychic and my prediction was going to come true before Marley spat the same three words out at our principal like acid.

"We. Didn't. Cheat."

Marley and our principal stared at each other for what felt like eons. Finally, Mr. Silby sat back down in his chair and massaged his temples. When he spoke again, he sounded tired, like Dad did after a really long day at the office.

"I've been doing this job for a long time, and I can tell when kids are lying. You two look just as shocked about your test scores as we are. So, I'm going to give you the benefit of the doubt here. Maybe you've turned new leaves. But. BUT. If I ever get the feeling you're not being honest about your schoolwork, you'll both have out-of-school suspension faster than you can blink. Are we clear?"

CHAPTER
FOUR

When school was out, Marley and I silently walked toward the line of idling school busses just outside the main entrance, both of us still processing the events of the day. I'd somehow escaped certain doom. I wanted nothing more than to go home, do my homework, and stare at my bedroom ceiling until sleep took me.

"Hold on, I want to try something," Marley blurted before dropping his backpack and running back up the stairs with his skateboard.

I knew what he was about to do, or try to do, rather. He'd spent all of last summer, and the summer before, trying to kickflip the set of five stairs in front of our school. Marley was a pretty good skateboarder, much better than I was, but he'd never come close to landing it. He must've tried it a thousand times.

Before I could tell Marley he'd get in trouble if a teacher saw him skating on school property, he was already rocketing toward the stairs. And then he was up in the air, effortlessly flicking his left foot out, resulting in the cleanest kickflip he'd ever pulled off. He stomped the landing as confidently as any professional skateboarder we'd seen in videos, rolling back toward me with a face-splitting grin. I remembered him telling me I looked the same, but I couldn't help but think he'd finally hit some kind of growth spurt because he looked, for lack of a better term, *thicker* than usual. I looked down at my arms. Marley clearly hadn't been paying attention, because I had two little bumps for biceps where before there had been nothing but skin and bone.

"I had to check to be sure." Marley said as he grabbed his backpack off the ground and strode for the bus. "Those kids. That thing. The Wheel. It was real, Caleb. It did something to us."

I've had many years to think about this series of events, and I can solidly conclude that this was moment my life really ended.

CHAPTER
FIVE

The three months that followed were filled with discovery. Marley and I independently explored the limits of the Wheel's boon, convening whenever possible to compare notes. What was most noticeable was that we both looked more attractive. Our acne cleared up almost instantly. We were both stronger and more agile, and studying for school was no longer necessary because we both just *knew* things if we concentrated hard enough. Much to Mr. Richter's dismay, we continued to ace his and all of our other seventh-grade classes, and I developed a reputation as quite the athlete.

But, as it turned out, we also came into individual skills which we didn't share. My ham-fisted notebook scribbles and short stories mutated into lavish works of professional-grade art. My parents, eager to facilitate a budding creative enthusiasm in their theretofore disappointing son, bought me a wide array of art supplies. Paints. Charcoals. Modeling clays. Canvasses. Even a big wooden easel. After a couple months, they splurged on a computer with a modem for schoolwork and design. I joined our school orchestra after sitting down with a cello, and nailing *Pachelbel's Canon in D Major* on the first try, without ever having looked at sheet music. Man, it felt good to have Mom and Dad feel proud of me, even if it wasn't really *my* talent.

Even if it came from an unearthly clearing in those dark woodlands that I knew with a wisdom exceeding my years I could never tell my parents about.

Marley, as I learned during one of our comparison meetings, still didn't have an artistic bone in his body. The Wheel's gift took him in an entirely different direction, one that imbued him with a heightened proficiency in manipulation. He'd con kids into handing over the desserts from their brown-bagged lunches, and had even managed to persuade a ninth-grade into giving him his mountain bike. His ability to finesse the people around him didn't stop at children. Teachers started giving him special privileges, allowing him to roam the halls without a bathroom pass, and even gave him permission to skateboard in front of the school whenever he wanted, landing impossible tricks to the applause of his new flock of adoring peers who started following him everywhere.

"It doesn't work on Dad, though." He told me on the school bus one day. "Mom is easy. I haven't done a single chore all week. Dad's a different story. Nothing I do can, like, fully charm him. I think I'm losing my mojo."

I nodded in agreement. By the end of that glorious three months, my paintings and playing were getting sloppier, and those long familiar Cs and Ds began trickling back into my report card, much to Mr. Richter's delight. Mom and Dad's frustration with me returned, and somehow made me feel even worse after that brief reprieve. I could only imagine what the mood was like at Marley's house.

I turned to watch golden foliage whizz past our window, hoping that would end the conversation. As the bus made the turn onto the long road which led to our neighborhood, I came to the conclusion that the Wheel didn't give us our gifts at random; it merely enhanced the parts of us that were the most *us*. It was the only explanation that made any sense. For me, it was art, because being creative made me feel good. For Marley, it was getting people to do things they didn't naturally want to do, because somehow that made him feel good.

"Caleb?" Marley was picking away at a hole in the green vinyl seat back in front of us.

"Yeah?"

"We have to go back. Back into the woods. We have to find it again."

I flinched. The adrenaline coursing through my body in the principal's office had finally ebbed, leaving me exhausted, virtually defenseless against a proposition so god damned insane. Still, I protested the best I could.

"Are you fucking crazy, Marley? Nun uh. Sorry man, I'm out."

Marley crammed his finger into the seat as he spoke, making the hole ever wider. "We have to see if we can get it back. We have to try."

I finally pried my eyes away from the window and looked at Marley. "Am I the only one who actually remembers that night? We barely made it out of there alive. Did you forget the giant fucking monster? Did you forget *we watched a little kid fucking get killed*? No man, we count our blessings. We try to pretend it never happened."

"We can't just go back to normal. You know that, right?"

Marley's eyes were wide. They were his desperation eyes, I knew. His scared eyes. He was two knuckles deep into the seat hole, revealing the piss-yellow cushion foam behind the green pebbled vinyl.

"I'm scared too. Fucking terrified, just like you are. What happened that night? That kid dying? It still gives me nightmares."

I remember experiencing the briefest flash of *Marley has never mentioned having a nightmare in his entire life* before he continued.

"You know how my dad is. It's bad enough at home with the powers, or whatever they are. But without them? I won't make it. I know I won't. I'll have to run away, or…I don't know. But even so, I'm not actually worried about me, here. I'm looking out for you."

"Me?"

"Yeah dude, *you*. Have you even *seen* yourself over the past couple weeks? Your art. It's insanely fucking good. Everyone loves it. You could make millions selling that shit. And the other stuff, too. You're getting straight as. You don't have a single zit on your face. And the girls? Don't think I didn't catch Mindy Macomb giving you make-out eyes in algebra the other day. You're a rock star. My best friend is a fucking *rock star*."

I blushed. Marley wasn't wrong. Before we got that boost in the woods, life was filled with insecurity and uncertainty. Everything was new. Everything was weird. It felt good to be appreciated by my peers for what felt like the first time in my short life. For the art I was creating. For my grades, my looks. Marley wasn't wrong about Mindy Macom either. Jesus. She'd been so far out of my league.

"It does feel good. But—"

"Of course it does, and it's not even the most important thing you're getting out of this. I've been over to your house a bunch since that night. The way your mom and dad talk to you? The way they look at you? They actually *like* you now, Caleb. They're proud of their son. That's why I want to go back out there, even though it's scary and dangerous and, friggin', like supernatural or whatever. You deserve to have parents who are proud of you."

As our bus slowed to a stop, I knew we were wrong to pinky swear we'd never go in those old woods again. There was no way we could simply resume our old, disappointing lives, at least not without having tried to figure out what we did wrong.

We would have to sneak back into the woodlands. Back to the clearing, the Wheel, the children, the place where a beautiful young girl had been liquefied by a leviathan made of flowers and moldering animal bones. And yet we still willingly risked our young lives by throwing them into very real peril because I didn't want to disappoint my best friend. I believed Marley knew me better than anyone, and if he thought I was unlovable and destined for unhappiness without that strange blessing from the woods, then it was all worth it. It had to be.

I grabbed my overstuffed backpack and scooted out into the bus aisle, past the cavernous hole Marley had torn into the seat back, past the pile of crumbled yellow stuffing on the floor.

THAT WEEKEND, Marley slept over at my house. Marley's dad had been on a real mean streak that week. That was fine with us, as it was easier to sneak out of my place anyway. Marley brought a backpack filled with flashlights, headlamps, bottles of water, trail mix, a first aid kit, and his old hand-drawn map of the woods, updated to include the general direction of where we'd found the Wheel. Mom made us pizza rolls for dinner, and we watched the Mortal Kombat movie in my bedroom, both of us only paying half attention. Our minds were focused on our plan of action after the house went dark, and we began hearing the snores coming from Mom and Dad's room.

"This is where it was." Marley insisted as we reached the area designated by a red crayon circle on his map. "I swear to God. It should be here."

We both looked around. There was no Wheel, no clearing. Not even a rocky hill. It was just more of the same old trees and brush and fallen logs.

"Yeah, this feels like the spot, but how the fuck does a hill disappear?"

"I don't know, Caleb. How does a giant floating Wheel and a monster made of forest trash disappear?" Marley was doing what he always did when he was frustrated, scoring points on me to make himself feel better.

We plunged ever deeper into the woodlands under Marley's lead, canvassing around the spot where the Wheel should have been in a half-mile radius, in case we'd been off by a little. There was nothing. We finally gave up just before sunrise. I climbed into my bed, still filthy and scratched up from pucker brush. Marley crawled into his crinkly G.I. Joe sleeping bag on the floor, back turned to me.

OUR BOOTS CRUNCHED through the leaf crust as we trudged in ever-widening circles in search of the Wheel. It had been four-and-a-half months since we'd first discovered it, and we'd had no luck finding it ever since. That mild autumn quickly careened into a brisk winter, forcing multiple layers and wool socks into what had developed into our efficient standard operating procedure.

"We're lost, aren't we."

Marley had his homemade map out, now almost overflowing with details and notes and frantic scribbles. "We're not lost, Caleb. I'm pretty sure I know exactly where we are."

"Did we not just pass this tree like an hour ago?" I shined my flashlight on an old maple tree, a frozen waterfall of crystalized sap cascading down one side of it. "I could've sworn we walked past this already."

Marley froze in his tracks, and slowly turned to meet my eyes. His face was red with rage.

"You think you can do better? Here, you take the map, smartass. You can lead for a change."

I extended my hand to take the map from my friend. "Why are you being a dick? I'd lead more often if you didn't insist on leading."

Marley quickly retracted the map before my gloved fingers could reach it.

"Because you're too stupid to do it right."

"What is your deal, man?"

"What is my deal, man?" Marley repeated my words back to me in the patronizing baby voice he always used when he was putting me down. "We just got a taste of something amazing, and now it's gone. That's my deal, Caleb. Whatever that was, I need to get it back. I need it."

"And we'll find it, Marley. We will. We'll find it eventually. We just have to be patient and— "

"I'd say you were a shitty friend if you were any friend at all. Fuck off, Caleb."

Marley stomped ahead into the darkness. I stood still, allowing him to create distance between us, trying to understand what I'd done wrong, and coming up with nothing that would make me feel better. The next morning, Marley showed up at the bus stop, all smiles and jokes.

"Hey", I said. "About last night."

"Oh that? That was nothing. Don't worry about it. Water under the bridge. Let's start planning for the next hike at lunch!"

THE BUSSES WERE RUNNING LATE, so my mom picked Marley and I up after school. Marley instantly snagged the passenger seat. I sat in the back, and drew little stick figures on the fogged-up windows as we made our way back to the cul-de-sac.

On the way home on the main road before we had to take a left that led us to the woodlands, those big golden arches of a McDonald's loomed in the near distance.

"Mom, can we stop for chicken nuggets?"

Mom sighed, and made eye contact with me through the rearview mirror. "Oh honey, I'm sorry. I don't want to spoil your dinner. Maybe next time, huh?"

"Did you know Caleb got an A+ on his math test today?" Marley said, fidgeting with the glove compartment button lock as he spoke.

I froze, trying to figure out what Marley was doing. We didn't have a test in math that day.

"He did?" Mom was shocked. She knew how much I struggled with math. With every subject, really, but math was the bane of my existence.

"He sure did! The only one in the class. Can you believe that? I think that's probably why he wanted to stop for McDonalds. To celebrate, you know?"

Mom gave me the proudest look I'd seen out of her since we had the Wheel's boon, and it made my heart ache.

"You know what?" Mom said as she put her blinker on to turn into the McDonalds parking lot. "That's a great idea. Let's celebrate that big A+! Way to go, Caleb!"

Marley turned around to face me in the backseat, and offered me a wink.

I REMEMBER it being one of those nights where it was too windy and cold for cloud cover. The stars were especially bright, and the moon was either a day early or a day late from being full, as there was a hint of a sliver missing that would have made it perfectly spherical. Marley and I trudged into the woodlands in full winter gear. Snow pants, boots, jackets, hats, and mittens. Thinking ahead, I'd asked Mom if I could make some cocoa for myself before bed, but had quietly poured it into a thermos that was stashed in my backpack.

Marley had his map out, and was once again consulting it to determine where we'd search. I knew Marley wasn't doing well, and really didn't want to suffer the blowback that would inevitably come if I chose to lead and we came up empty handed again, but I just couldn't do it anymore. I'd let him be in charge the previous three months because it was easier than listening to him sulk when it was the other way around, but it had gotten us nowhere. I was honestly a little surprised by how strong my feelings were about it. It was like I'd been holding a grudge against him for a slight I didn't even understand, and without even knowing I was holding it.

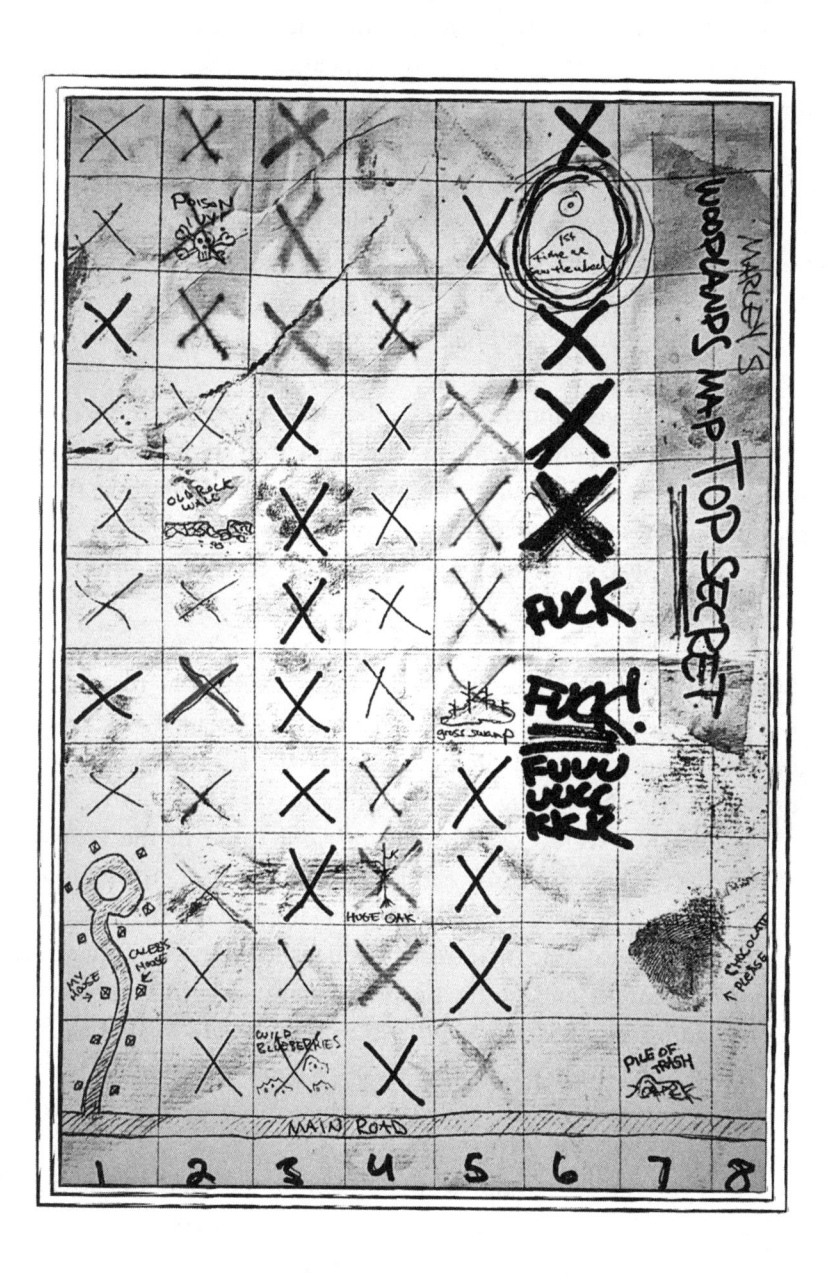

I crunched past him as he was penciling in a projected area for us to explore. He hollered at me to slow down, doing his best to fold his map and follow me at the same time. I meandered this way and that, allowing my heart to decide the route instead of my brain.

"We're not gonna find anything this way, Caleb! You're an idiot!" Marley huffed and puffed behind me, his labored breath coming out in big frozen clouds. I trudged forward, blissfully meandering this way and that, ignoring Marley's pleas.

"Fuck you, Marley. I found it the first time, and—"

And before I could even finish the sentence, I'd found it the second time.

Marley and I were moving so fast that we almost ran into the base of the rocky hill. There it was, the large clearing, those angelic children's singing voices, that technicolor night sky, the moon that, on top of being perfectly round and full, was entirely too big.

And the Wheel, scoured of gore since we'd last seen it, gleaming in the moonlight.

We scrambled up the hill as quickly as we could, both of us worried it would all disappear again if we didn't act fast enough. Tufts of lush green grass and wildflowers rushed past me, and the pleasant summer breeze dried my sweat as I climbed. Seasons weren't the same in proximity to the Wheel.

This time, we were greeted by a different Child of the Wheel, a boy that was maybe seven or eight. He had freckles, and his brown hair was shaved down the middle of his skull, leaving his remaining hair in a wavy cascade that reached his shoulders. His grin was warm and genuine, and he held a pair of white nightgowns out for us. We shed our winter gear, leaving it in individual sweaty heaps as we slipped into the cool, clean gowns without hesitation. Marley, perennially insecure about his body, turned away as from us as he changed.

"I'm sorry for what happened to your friend, and I'm sorry if Marley and I running away offended you." I said to the young boy.

"I am happy to see you. You needn't worry about those who go willingly to the Wheel. We all are called to it eventually."

"That monster," Marley said, a noticeable quaver in his voice as he scanned the hilltop for it. "The thing made out of bones and sticks. Tell us about that, please."

The young boy smiled. "Monster? Oh, you mean Old Friend. You needn't worry about him, either. He is an automaton, sent to us by our Master, and only does what She asks of it."

His answer didn't seem to do much for Marley's nerves, but I was satisfied with the young boy's response. If he wasn't scared of it, I didn't think we needed to be scared of it either.

"Please, join us for The Ritual of the Wheel. I understand you have questions. All will become clear. You will see."

Marley and I did as we were asked. The enormous Wheel thrummed as it spun faster than human eyes could register, and I was again enveloped in that wholesome sense of well-being and strength and potential. We clasped our clammy hands together, and sung the Hymn of Demelae. I watched as the swirling nebulae and twinkling stars gave way to the gaping black maw that led to the entity's domain.

A crunch coming from the bottom of the hill signaled the return of Old Friend. Marley and I looked at each other as we sang, both of us believing in our hearts we were playing a game of Russian roulette, and that Old Friend could potentially choose one of us to be ground into a nourishing paste. This time we didn't turn around as we felt its heavy steps shake the hill under our bare feet. To this day, I don't ever believe I've ever felt more excited or terrified.

Old Friend summitted the hill, its moose skull caked in flesh so black and decayed it was nearly mulch, and once again clasped its hands together in praise of the children, the Wheel, and the thing beyond the amorphous black hole that was its master. I clenched my eyes shut, sending tears rolling down my cheeks as I did my best to keep from hyperventilating. It was almost time for a Child of the Wheel to be pulped on the Wheel, and I wanted to run again. What were we doing? We had our whole lives ahead of us, so why were we casually gambling them? What if it picked me? Would Marley even try to stop it, or would he just claim his powers, and tell my parents I must've run away?

Unclenching its giant, thorny claws, Old Friend made slow, striding circles around the Wheel, a grotesque imitation of duck, duck, goose. It seemed as if it were parsing out which child was the best possible candidate for sacrifice.

When it was directly behind Marley and I, Old Friend stopped moving. I looked at Marley. He was quaking so violently I thought he was going to collapse. Like before when we first encountered Old Friend, I felt a hot jet of urine stream down my bare leg. One of us was going to die. I heard the creak of saplings bowing under heavy snow as Old Friend bent to make its selection. I gulped. Marley shook. We never stopped singing.

The vinous, unwavering fingers of Demelae's avatar curled around the boy next to me; the freckled one who'd welcomed us back to the Wheel, and given us our robes. I wanted to cry out in protest, but the boy simply smiled at me, and said, "You don't have to worry. To be chosen, you must go willingly. I accept this. I want this. It is a good thing."

Knowing the order of events did nothing to quell my fear or outrage. My mind reeled as Old Friend brought the boy in for a loving embrace, just as he had the first time we'd experienced the ritual.

Why do you want this? I wanted to scream as the young boy hugged his murderer, even though I knew I was standing there because I wanted to receive the boon from one of their sacrifices. *How could you possibly want this?* But I was powerless to do anything but clasp my hands, and sing, and watch in horror as Old Friend gradually positioned the boy head-first toward the whirling monstrosity, and drew him closer.

He never stopped smiling until the whine of that nightmare Wheel ground his jaw down to the stub of his neck.

Liquefied viscera coated the Wheel's relentless edge, and rocketed up, up into the sky, where it disappeared into the hole to be consumed by an unseen creature. My misfiring mind created a cartoonish image of a multi-limbed Hindu god using a butter knife to slather it on a piece of toast before the wholesome sensation of the Wheel kicked into overdrive. I shivered in ecstasy as it flowed over and through me. There was no part of me that wasn't bathed in the Wheel's euphoric blessing. I didn't know if what we were experiencing was some kind of energy released from the boy's body, a power shed from the Wheel as it converted him into gruel, or a gift that came directly from the being beyond the black hole, and at that moment, I didn't care.

Finished with its task, Old Friend withdrew from the Wheel. The singing stopped, and the intense sensation ebbed enough for me to look down, and realize I had a throbbing erection. I covered myself with my hands and turned to Marley, who was dealing with the same issue. The Children of the Wheel all waved goodbye to us, and made their way down the rocky hill, disappearing into the thick brush below.

Old Friend stopped for a moment to stare at Marley and me with its vacant eye sockets, and then pointed in the direction of our neighborhood with one long arm. Its message was clear. *Time for you to go home.* We quickly changed back into our winter wear and scurried down the hill just as the first snowflakes of the storm started to fall.

I thought I'd be awake forever. Adrenaline still pumped through me as I quietly slipped back into my room, and crawled into bed. But sleep came eventually, long and deep and dreamless.

As I SHOVELED our driveway that afternoon, I realized the Child of the Wheel had been right. All *did* become clear. Participating in the ritual from start to finish had somehow imbued us with innate knowledge that felt more like old memories than newly acquired information.

The Children of the Wheel were not from here, but they weren't alien visitors from another world, either. Marley and I were the ones doing the traveling. The Wheel was much more than just a sacrificial altar, its mechanism responsible for why their world touched ours. Either way, when Marley and I communed with the Children of the Wheel, it wasn't on Earth.

I felt my heart thrumming in my chest with a gloved hand, experiencing the new and almost nauseating tingle inside me, pulling me directly towards the woodlands. I had no doubt, at the end of that tingle, I'd find the Wheel again. It had gifted me with a compass, and hoped we'd use it.

CHAPTER
SIX

Once during the winter of our collage senior year we had to drive home for a family emergency. Marley's Aunt Susan, his father's sister, had been hit by a boat propeller while vacationing in Bermuda, and her body had been transported to the funeral home down the road from our neighborhood. I remember the roads were awful on the way up because of an ice storm, and even at a crawling pace we were still sliding all over the highway. It ended up taking us four hours to complete the one hour drive, and by the time we'd parked we grabbed our bags and went to our respective parents' houses, too exhausted and frazzled to even say goodbye to each other.

Mom and Dad were thrilled to see me, as always. Mom had spent the day making a huge lasagna to ensure her son was properly fed after months of garbage college cafeteria food. I swear I ate half of that thing while Mom and Dad peppered me with questions about my grades, my plans for after college, and about my dating life.

"You want to know about girls, you might want to ask Marley instead of me. That kid is a regular Hugh Heffner."

Dad cackled. "I love it. You know, I never thought Marley would end up being a ladies man. He was always so, I don't know."

"Weird." Mom said, and then we all cackled together.

I crawled into my old bed shortly after, and was dozing when my phone chirped. Marley was texting me.

M-DAWG: We should hit the Wheel while we're up here. Just about ready for a refill anyway.

CALEB: Yeah man, for sure. Probably can't swing it tomorrow with the funeral, but maybe the day after?

M-DAWG: Sounds good.

CALEB: Hey, how are you holding up over there? Is your Dad behaving?

I waited for a response, but it never came. Eventually I fell asleep.

I woke up and Mom was already ironing my dress clothes for the funeral. I told her she didn't need to but she insisted, saying it was a treat for her because she never got to take care of her baby boy anymore. Dad was already in his suit eating breakfast at the kitchen table. They'd both known Marley's aunt and were still close with his parents, so they were coming to the funeral too. They said there weren't going to be a lot people in attendance because Marley's family wasn't very tight and there weren't many of them around.

When I was showered and dressed, I texted Marley to see if he was already there.

M-DAWG: Yeah, I'm here. Place is a ghost town. Pun intended. Wanna sit with me up front?

CALEB: Of course dude.

We got to the funeral home an hour later, and I remember feeling sad about how few cars were in the parking lot. I knew Marley's family wasn't close like ours because I grew up watching him celebrate all the major holidays with just his parents, but it was another thing to see it visually represented like that. It made me think about how undiluted Marley's relationship with his mom and dad must've been because outside of me and schoolwork there was really no distraction caused by any other presences in his life. It was just *them*. I think it made me understand him a little better than I already did.

I took off my pea coat when we got inside, and was promptly

greeted by Marley's parents. Marley's mom looked thin. Too thin. It was that wiry-yet-strong kind of body my grandma had because, instead of dealing with whatever gave her anxiety (read: Grandpa's love of Wild Turkey), she just constantly did chores and cooked. She was like a shark that would die if it didn't stop swimming. Only Marley's mom was way too young to be looking like that. It worried me.

"Hey, there's the big bucko!" Marley's dad slapped my shoulder with his baseball glove of a hand. "How the hell are you?"

"I'm good. I'm sorry for your loss."

"Thanks, Caleb. I swear I must've told Sue to be careful on those Caribbean diving excursions of hers a thousand times."

I was used to people being gregarious at funerals because that was a New England thing, but there was usually a noticeable undercurrent of grief and loss. Marley's dad exhibited none of that. He acted like us talking was a chance encounter in a supermarket aisle, and not like his only sister's casket was fifty paces away.

"Yeah" I said. "That's so sad."

Marley blessedly materialized in the foyer. He was wearing an incredibly fancy black suit. I didn't know anything about fashion brands then, but even I could tell that thing must've been wildly expensive. I remember looking down at my untailored jacket and ill-fitting dress shirt and feeling very insecure about how I looked next to him.

"Hey dude", Marley said.

"Hey", I said back. "How are you doing, man?"

"He's fine" Marley's dad interrupted. "Clearly more concerned with looking like a mafia don than with his aunt's passing. You and I? We're dressed *respectably* for an event like this."

Marley's mom walked over with a tray of cheese cubes and tooth-picks; undoubtedly playing her role as chief situation diffuser. "Here, you growing boys need to eat!"

I sat in the front pew with Marley during the service. My mom and dad were a few pews behind us, and the handful of Marley's relatives were scattered around both sides of the aisle. A reverend from the Congregational church offered some Bible verses and a prepared speech about the life and times of Aunt Susan. The casket was in front of him and to the left, closed due to the extent of the injuries that had put her in it.

Marley's mom and dad sat at the opposite end of our pew. I remember being distracted by his dad's perpetually bouncing knee. It was as if he couldn't wait to get out of there because he had somewhere better to be. Occasionally his mother would place a hand on his knee in an effort to stop it, but Marley's dad would just brush it off and continue bouncing.

"For lack of better phrasing, Susan was a *liver of life*. She was active in her community, traveled extensively around the globe, and was loved by many, as we…um, can see here."

I couldn't help but think the reverend had prepared that line long before he realized how empty the room was going to be.

"She was an avid dancer, diver, and…"

The reverend paused to take a sip from a water bottle he'd stashed away inside the dais.

"…And was extremely fond of animals. She…"

He trailed off again, and I couldn't help but feel like something was off. I slowly cocked my head to look around the room, and nobody seemed to notice or be bothered by it.

"She…she…was also a piece of shit."

I gasped. I didn't even try to hide it when I scanned the room a second time to gauge people's reactions to a man of god swearing at a funeral service. Mom and Dad weren't making faces of disgust. One person cleared their throat. Marley's dad let out a chuckle. Otherwise they just stared ahead as if nothing was wrong. I started wondering if I'd heard him incorrectly; that he'd said *piece of work*, which was still off but not outright insane.

The reverend continued. "At this point we'd like to invite members of the family to share their memories of Susan and pay their respects."

Someone from the back of the room, I'm pretty sure it was one of

Marley's third cousins on his mom's side or something like that, stood and walked to the dais. He had a buzz cut and it made me think he was in law enforcement.

"First I'd like to thank everyone for showing up today. I know the weather hasn't been cooperating, but it's good to see us all gathered together to send Susan off."

I settled back into my seat, convinced my ears had just been playing tricks on me, and listened.

"Gosh, what can I say about Susan that hasn't already been said about Amy Winehouse? My god did that woman eat pills like they were Tic Tacs."

Marley's dad let out a bark of laughter. A few other chuckles sounded from around the room. I spun around. Mom and Dad were grinning like idiots.

"Hell yeah she did! Probably why her head got turned into Hamburger Helper by that boat prop!" Said a relative I'd never met before, resulting in even more laughter.

Suddenly I knew what was going on. I looked at Marley, and saw a trickle of sweat dripping down the side of his face.

"What the hell are you doing, dude?"

Marley just stared ahead, and spoke through his gritted teeth. He was clearly pushing his power hard, maybe harder than I'd ever seen before. "I'm just taking the brakes off their brains and letting them say what they really think about her. Shut up and enjoy the show."

"Anyway", his third cousin continued, "Fuck her, and good riddance."

Several people clapped, including Marley's dad.

"Wait, I thought you said you couldn't push your dad."

"I'm not. That's literally just who he is."

I was stunned into silence by that. The third cousin left the dais, and Aunt Susan's husband approached. I sat frozen in anticipation of what he was about to say.

"I've actually had a separate family for almost a decade. Kept it from her the entire time. They live down in Connecticut, and every time I said I was travelling for work I was actually being a husband and father to people I just like way more. I'm glad she's dead."

The reverend hopped out of his chair behind the dais and clapped. "Hear hear! I've only met her a handful of times over the years but she was truly vile, wasn't she! Hope you buy your second family something nice with that insurance money!"

I felt like I was going to puke on my shoes. It was all too much.

"I hated her too!" I turned around. It was my mother speaking. "She was so rude and my god, those slide shows she'd make us suffer through were *the worst*."

I grabbed Marley's arm, hard. "You need to cut the shit right now. Not me. Not my parents. Ever. That was the deal."

Marley finally looked away from the front of the room and at me. He was dripping sweat and his bloodshot eyes bulged with rage and frustration.

"IT'S MY FAMILY, CALEB." Marley screamed into my face. "IT'S MINE TO DO WHATEVER I WANT WITH IT. IT'S MINE."

"Oh my god, what is happening? I feel dizzy."

It was my mom in the back. My dad hand his hands on her shoulders and looked extremely concerned. I looked around the room, and everyone was slumped over. Some held their heads in anguish. Others clutched their stomachs. I'd realize later that Marley's spell had been broken by my interference, and that he wouldn't speak to me for weeks over it.

The reverend said "I don't feel so hot" and then collapsed.

Everyone evacuated the funeral home. Marley and I didn't speak for a couple weeks after that. Later the episode would be blamed on a natural gas leak, and everyone who attended Aunt Susan's funeral would say how lucky we all were that the building didn't blow up while we were still in it.

Marley and I had continued to visit the Wheel throughout high school and college. Like clockwork, our boons would begin to fade around the three-month mark, at which point we'd make the trek out to the woods for a refill. Also like clockwork, I'd suffer regular breakdowns about feeling forced to witness that awful brutality just to keep my life on a positive trajectory, and insist I didn't want to do it anymore. I had nightmares, and my appetite all but disappeared. I was traumatized.

Of course, Marley remained largely unphased by the Ritual of the Wheel, and always found a way to talk me back into another round. *Just one more time. Do it for me. Do it for you. Do it for your Mom and Dad.* He'd pick away at me until he hit just the right pain point, and then I'd be right back out there. After a while, pretending the horrors I was witnessing was nothing but self-care became a ritual in itself; me protesting, Marley massaging my fragile emotional state until I felt better about the awful thing we both knew I was going to say yes to anyway. Eventually the nightmares stopped, as did my protestations. Something I learned during this time that it becomes very hard to purposefully make yourself uncomfortable after you've lived comfortably for too long. At that point I'd built too much of my life using the Wheel's boon as my foundation. Regardless of Marley's manipulations, I couldn't go back to life without a cheat code, so I made concessions and rationalized and disassociated and became emotionally dishonest with myself; whatever it took to keep it all going.

As the years progressed, we needed to visit the Wheel more often to stay powered up. Whether it was because we were developing a tolerance or merely because we were getting older, we had no idea. We were also clueless as to how there could possibly be a ritual to attend whenever we happened to need one, or why the pale granite of the Wheel had been slowly darkening to a mildew grey over the years. Marley had never felt pressured to know more about the ritual, and at the age of twenty-one even I was beyond trying to understand it. All we knew was that we went every three months back in junior high, upped it to ever two months in high school, and by the time we started college, we were attending the Ritual of the Wheel about once a month.

On the day we graduated college, Marley and I were both primed and ready. We'd shot through our respective curriculums with ease, and both earned enough accolades and dean's list to perk the ears of our future employers. My work with mixed media paintings at Harvard Arts had piqued the interest of several trendy New York galleries, as well as emails from a talent agency rep. Marley was already rich by the time we hit senior year. He'd started several businesses that were filling his bank account without him lifting a finger, and he was due to start working at a financial firm in the city a week after receiving his diploma.

Dressed in our graduating gowns, we sat on empty football bleachers, sharing a joint as we watched a team of men arrange chairs for the ceremony on the field.

"We're finally doing it," I said as I exhaled a heroic cloud of smoke. "New York City, baby. It's gonna be awesome!"

Marley's text alert dinged in his pocket as he pinched the joint from my fingers. "Hell yeah. We're gonna have a hell of a time. Making money, scoring babes, living that big city life. We're gonna kill it. Plus we just had that last top off at the Wheel. All systems are go, brother."

"Yeah we are. We're—"

Marley's text alert interrupted me. He rolled his eyes, and reached into his pocket as a flurry of dings came in all at once.

"Jesus, who the hell is that?"

"Ugh, it's nothing. It's just Becky."

Becky was the girl he was casually dating at the time. She was drop dead gorgeous, and a genuinely nice person. We both knew if it weren't for Marley's supercharged charm and good looks she wouldn't have given him a second glance.

"What's up with her? She OK?"

"Oh yeah, she's fine. I'm just waiting for her to break up with me."

I coughed mid-toke, and looked at him. "What are you talking about? I thought you guys were good."

"We are good," Marley said. "But we're heading out to NYC. I don't want that kind of baggage when we hit the city. I want to play the field."

"I don't know, man. She's a total catch. You sure you don't want to try and make things work?"

Marley raised a finger to his lips as to shush me. He stared at his phone as three more text alert dings came through. "Aaaannnnd it's done."

"What's done?"

"Becky and I. She finally gave up."

"Gave up?"

"Yeah, I'd didn't feel like going through all the trouble of breaking it off myself, so I just acted like an asshole until she gave up and dumped me."

I looked at my best friend as if for the first time. "I'm sorry, but why didn't you just break up with her like a normal human being?"

"Like I said, I didn't feel like it. Why use my power all the time when I can just let things, I don't know, fix themselves?"

I didn't know how to respond to that. It felt so cruel and strange. It was less like a breakup, and more like he was throwing out an empty can of soda.

Marley cut in before I could respond. "Oh hey, we have to talk. We'll still need to hit the Wheel every month. You have any plan for how you're going to do that?"

I didn't have any idea how I was going to do that. I couldn't afford to travel to New Hampshire once a month. I was so nervous about having to skip visits to the Wheel and losing my edge that I almost wanted my opportunity in New York to fall through. The thought of achieving everything I'd worked toward for four years only to fail the minute I'd gotten it was too much for me. It had been keeping me up at night for weeks.

"Yeah, I had a feeling. Listen, I'll pay for your apartment as well as our airfare back and forth."

I cried a little in relief, and humbly accepted.

"Of course, Caleb. Money isn't a big deal for me anymore. Might as well spend it. And besides, us *Wheel Kids* gotta stick together, right?"

"Wheel Kids", I repeated as I plucked the roach from his fingers. "That has an excellent ring to it."

CHAPTER
SEVEN

The years flew by, as they do.

Four years after arriving in New York City, I'd founded the top art gallery in New York, which had three locations spread across the city. It was all funded by Marley, who was then being referred to as "The Rasputin of Wall Street" by Forbes Magazine, but it was my notoriety as an artist that made the gallery a viable business. I'd grown it to the point that I had a hierarchy of managers running the show, which left me time to paint, curate, give interviews to various media outlets, and spend time with my family.

I met my wife Claudia on social media. She'd commented on a mutual friend's post, and her profile picture made me drop everything and learn all about her from what she'd written in her "About Me" section. She lived in the city, and worked as a librarian. When I saw she was originally from New Hampshire, and that she'd listed my favorite bar as her favorite bar (a dimly lit British pub called The Coat of Arms), I messaged her with the corniest line imaginable.

If your favorite bar really is The Coat of Arms, I will put a ring on your finger.

She laughed, and we started talking. Five years of dating later, and I made good on my promise. Two years after that, we gave birth to our oldest daughter, Quinn, and two years after that, we added our youngest daughter Dee-Dee to the litter. By the time I was forty-one years old, I was a successful artist, owned a business I was truly passionate about, became a husband to the greatest woman I've ever known, and a father to two beautiful, intelligent girls. I had life by the balls, and I was grateful for every second of it.

In fact, I was successful enough that I started skipping trips to the Wheel. First it was one visit, then two. I'd skate by for a while on things I'd done before the boon expired, but never for too long. If I waited too long, things started falling apart. An investment would go to shit, or I'd screw up an important gallery event. I'd even look worse physically. Claudia would say I looked tired. Stooped. When I saw the failure cracks starting to spider web out into everything, I'd give in and join my best friend in the woods to re-up at the Wheel, which at that point had turned mottled and blotchy and had developed a slight wobble. But those months when I wasn't forced to watch a child turn into soup to keep my life propped up? Those were good months. Weightless, wonderful months. I tried to go for longer and longer each time. This time, it'd been two months, and I was barely hanging on. Even my therapist had quit on me. And that's when Marley showed up, like he knew, on a rainy Tuesday at the gallery.

Marley announced that he was taking me on an impromptu trip back home. As always, he was dressed to the nines in a custom tailored Gucci suit, and boasted a wide, impossibly white smile. "I have a surprise for you." He said. "I think you're gonna love it."

"I can't just abandon my kids on a whim, Marley." There was no way I could have told him having children of my own had dredged up all my repressed guilt about what I profited from at the Wheel, and how it had mutated me into quite the helicopter parent. It still made me cringe to think about when Claudia sent Dee-Dee to her room for cutting the tails off her My Little Pony dolls, and I spent the night playing with her up there because I didn't want her to feel lonely. Claudia was furious, and said I was undermining her authority. If she couldn't understand, Marley *never* would have understood.

"Don't worry about it. I sprung for an all-expenses paid vacation to

St. Maarten for Claudia and the girls to keep them busy while we're gone."

"Jesus Christ, Marley. Did you not think to ask me before you did that? Fine. I'll ask Claudia if she minds. If I find out you tried working your manipulation mojo on her to get your way, I'll rip your throat out like Patrick Swayze in Road House."

He laughed, and feigned mock consternation. "Me? Manipulate someone? I can't believe you'd say something like that."

The Wheels of Marley's private jet touched down in New Hampshire that evening. After deplaning, we hustled ourselves into a chauffeured Bentley idling on the tarmac. A copy of that day's Washington Post lay in the backseat. A flattering paparazzi photo of Marley was printed under the headline ABUSIVE BILLIONAIRE SKATES ON FRAUD CHARGES. Marley was always in the paper for one thing or another. It was either a paparazzi shot of him walking into Chateau Marmont with an A-list actress, or him being accused of some kind of corporate malfeasance. I didn't have details about the story behind that headline and I didn't share Marley's business acumen, but I was sure he did it, whatever *it* was.

"Jesus Christ, Marley. How much money *do* you make?"

Marley laughed, and looked out the window. "Enough to do what I'm about to show you."

"Where have you been lately, by the way?" I asked him as I looked at my phone. "I sent you a text about Dee-Dee's birthday party two weeks ago, and you never bothered to answer."

"I've been busy. Mom's staying at the apartment for a week."

I grimaced.

OUT OF ALL Marley's strange quirks and bad habits, Marley's relationship with his mother was near the top of my *ick list*. Even as an adult in his thirties, his mother insisted on coddling him. Marley delighted in it, and applied his own pressure to it over the years, mutating it into something that went well beyond unhealthy parenting. I'll never forget the day I called Marley back after several missed calls, only for him to tell me to hold on a second. He must've forgotten to mute his phone before he put it down, because I could hear him yelling at someone.

"Mom, what the fuck. Where are the canapes? The guests are complaining?"

I had to stifle a gasp to keep Marley from realizing I was still on the other line. He'd only said a handful of words, but I immediately knew what was happening. He was clearly flying his mother from New Hampshire to Manhattan so she could dote on him in his high-rise penthouse as if he were just a helpless kid who wasn't yet allowed to use the home appliances. He could afford a legion of maids and assistants and butlers, but there he was, screaming at his elderly mother to serve hors d'oeuvres at one of his parties like some kind of abused donkey. The thought of it made me nauseous.

"The toast points are almost ready to come out of the oven, kiddo!"

"Is Dad coming?"

"I'm sorry, baby. He said he's not going to make it tonight because he's doing some kind of historic waterfront tour in the city. You know how he loves those old boats."

"My private jet was good enough for him to fly on, but *I'm* not good enough for him to make an appearance?"

I couldn't help but feel sad for him in that moment. Even after a lifetime of abuse and neglect from his father, and after all of his success in life, he was still so desperate for that vile old man's approval.

"What do you want from me? He is who he is!"

I could *feel* Marley's rage vibrating in the handful of seconds before he answered. "Right, and who he is is a terrible husband and father who you would have left ages ago if you weren't so god damned codependent."

"Oh, the toast points are ready!"

"For fuck's sake, you're not even listening. You've never listened to me a single day in your entire life. Neither of you have. I fucking hate both of you. You think this party is big? Wait for the one I throw when the two of you kick the bucket."

"Gonna run the dishwasher real quick!"

There was a rustling noise, and then a brief pause before Marley once again spoke into his phone.

"Oh shit, I forgot to actually put you on hold. Whoops!"

"You did?" I said, wondering if Marley's powers meant he could sense deception over a cellular signal. "I wasn't even paying attention. Just sitting here watching Dee-Dee build a Lego fortress."

"AND HEY", Marley said, "It's not like you never ignore my texts. Glass houses, yadda yadda."

"Seventeen missed texts about me needing to drop everything to hop on a cruise, or join you for a red carpet event five minutes before it starts? Come on, man. I have a wife and kids. You know I can't swing that."

"So you just don't answer?"

"It's fucking hard to say no to you, Marley. If I answer and say no, you won't stop until I say yes. It's relentless, and it sucks. So yes, sometimes I just don't answer. Sometimes I don't want to spend all night going back and forth with you while you try to cajole me into something I don't want to do."

"...So it's OK when you don't answer, but it's not OK when I don't answer. Got it."

"Jesus Christ, Marley. You blow up my phone with texts wanting to hang out on night I absolutely can't, and then I don't hear from you for a month. It's like you only think of me when you need something, and it sucks."

"Whatever, Caleb. You're just being a baby."

Being Marley's best friend didn't feel like anything else in my life. In anyone's life probably. He was someone that made you feel like you were the only person in the world who mattered. Hanging out with Marley was always an electric experience. I absolutely cherished any and all time we spent together up until it started becoming more of a chore than a blessing. I'd end up staring at a basketball game on a bar television for hours as Marley ignored me, engrossed in the act of juggling several different Instagram conversations with ex-girlfriends as if it was nothing but a video game, making each of them feel uniquely special and wanted just long enough to send him a lewd photo, or invite him over. Every other night I'd end up being responsible for getting him back to his luxury apartment building's doorman safely when he inevitably got too drunk. After a while, I felt like more like his butler than I did his friend.

Eventually, I had to make a conscious decision to strike a healthier balance in my personal life. When Marley would invite me to a high-end strip club or a quick trip to San Tropez, I'd counter with an invite to dinner at my place. I'd offer to make him meatballs using my mother's recipe which he loved growing up, and said the wife and kids would enjoy spending time with their Uncle Marley. This was a slight fabrication, as the kids loved their Uncle Marley, but my wife, who felt Marley resented her for taking up time and attention that should be lavished on him alone, only put up with him because he was my life-long best friend. He'd always decline, citing a last-minute business issue, or that he'd forgotten he had a pre-existing date with some exotic runway model. With Marley, there was no compromise. No plan B. Social plans had to be on his terms, or there were no terms at all.

The Bentley pulled into the cul-de-sac less than an hour later and parked in the street between our houses. The street lights were on, as were the lights at our parents' places, but the rest of the neighborhood was blacked out. It was only 8:30 pm, so it wasn't like the neighbors were all asleep or anything.

"What, did you send everyone else on a vacation, too?"

"Something like that", Marley said as he tried to control the trickster's grin spreading on his face. "I bought the entire neighborhood."

Marley had his hands in just about every financial pie you could imagine. Investments, property management, venture capital, franchise ownership, restaurants, hotels, race horses. If it made money, Marley used his talents to shoehorn his way into it. After watching the cherished public park next to his office building turn into condos, he had the team running his real estate holdings crunch some numbers regarding housing scarcity in New England. Green spaces and conservation areas were being sold off to developers at an alarming rate. His projections showed it was only a matter of time before the stuffed suits running sleepy old New Hampshire weighed the pros and cons of peeling swathes of conservation land off to developers in favor of more housing for younger, gainfully employed families looking to escape city life in Boston and New York, who would, in turn, fill the state's coffers with much needed tax money.

"So...you bought the entire neighborhood? Because of some projections?"

"I sure did. I made cash offers to everyone on the street, triple what everything was actually worth. Even old man Grimford at the end of the turnaround took the money. I figured he'd hold out until the earth spiraled into the sun. Not your parents' place, though. I know they're leaving that to you, anyway. Not my parents either. There isn't a figure I could throw at Dad to make him leave."

"But why? That must've cost you—"

"Twelve houses for just under thirty million dollars. Also sprung for movers to quietly clear each house out in the dead of night, as to not worry the 'rents. Made all the neighbors sign NDAs while I was at it."

I leaned against the mailbox I'd spent nearly forty years fetching bills and birthday cards from. I felt dizzy. The beautiful little neighborhood I'd spent my childhood in had just been felt dead, and empty. Marley had scooped everything up so secretly and tidily that even my parents who lived there hadn't known about any of it. They'd have called to tell me the neighbors were moving out all at once.

"Yeah, it was a lot of money, but nowhere near as much as it cost to buy the woodlands along with it. That set me back a cool quarter bill."

A cool quarter bill. It took my artist's brain a moment to decode what he was saying; a quarter of a billion dollars.

"You...you spent two hundred and fifty million?!"

"On the woodlands, yes. Give or take. But don't forget the thirteen million for the neighborhood. Oh, and all of that god damned fencing. I think I spend another twenty-four mill on fencing."

"Fencing." I was just repeating bits of what Marley was saying at that point. I needed a drink. I needed ten drinks.

"Yeah, seventy-four miles of electrified chain link fence isn't cheap. Neither is the razor wire topper! But I figured it made sense. The government was in charge of keeping people from fucking around in the woodlands before. Now it's up to us to protect the once-protected woodlands, now that it's just a massive chunk of private property."

"Us?"

"Yeah, man. Us. You thought I dragged you all the way up here just to gloat about burning five percent of my net worth? I love forcing you to have fun, but that's more of an email."

"Why did you do this, Marley?"

"We need the woodlands. The woodlands were in danger. I bought the woodlands. Now the woodlands aren't in danger anymore. Weird way to say 'Thank you, Marley. That was very generous and thoughtful of you, Marley.'"

"Why did you buy the neighborhood, too?"

"Every person living on this street was a liability to our interests, Caleb. Securing it was always going to part of the package. You want randos stumbling up to that Wheel and getting hurt?"

"So what, are you just going to blockade the neighborhood? Leave it empty? What are our parents supposed to do? You just made sure they live in a ghost town."

"I don't need to be in the city anymore. You don't need to be in the city anymore. Everything we do can be done remotely. Your parents keep talking about moving to Florida. You said Claudia always wanted to move back to New Hampshire eventually—"

"You're fucking kidding me."

"I'm not fucking kidding you. Let's move back home. It's time."

"It's time? Who the fuck are you to tell me it's time?! I've literally never been happier, Marley. Not that you ever gave a shit about that. My life is the best it's ever been. Claudia. Dee-Dee. Quinn. The gallery. The city. I finally wake up in the morning, and sometimes my heart isn't even full of regret."

"Regret? What, because of the Children of the Wheel? You owe everything good in your life to what happens in those woods, but now, thirty years later, you're concerned about how the sausage is made?

"What if I am?"

"Give me a fucking break, Caleb. You know what? Fine. Go ahead and stop visiting the Wheel."

"I fucking will. Watch me."

"Good. Let your boon expire. I'll give you a month of normalcy before you're dangling from the end of an extension cord noose. I know that's where I'd be if I had to stop living like this."

"How does it not bother you?"

"I don't know, because I'm practical?"

"Why do you think I've been taking those breaks, Marley? There's something deeply wrong with you if you can watch kids take part in ritual human sacrifice for as long as we have without it affecting you. There's something dead inside you, man. I think you might need some help."

It felt like someone outside of my body far wiser than I am was saying the words. *I think you might need some help.* Like the sentiment was bubbling up from somewhere deep in my subconscious that I actively refused to explore.

"They want it!" Marley raised his voice, just as I knew he would after even the slightest amount of criticism. "They want it! They go willingly! They're fucking smiling as it happens! And you're smiling as you reap the benefits, even if you do skip a few rounds to perform your little Good Guy Caleb cosplay for an audience of one. And I'll tell you another thing. Those little breaks you take are putting your entire life at risk. Don't think I haven't seen how much your shit crumbles when you stop."

"Are you even capable of looking past your own interests for long enough to realize they're kids? They're just little kids out there, Marley! They can't possibly know what they want!"

"We don't know how any of this shit works, Caleb. Even now, after all these years. We're just as in the dark about how or why any of it happens as we were the first night we stumbled onto it. We don't know why we have keep visiting it more often as time goes on, or why it's been changing color or wobbling, or any of that shit. All you and I know for sure is that everything goes away if we stop going to the Wheel. That's why I did what I did, and I didn't tell you about it precisely because of how you're reacting now."

"Oh, that's great. What a nice guy you are. Always looking out for my best interests. Saint Marley of Selfless Street. And hey, I guess your mom won't have to travel as far to scrub your underwear anymore. That's a plus."

"You need to stop looking at this as a curse, and start looking at this for what it really is. It's an opportunity, Caleb. An opportunity for us to live our best possible lives. An opportunity for our families to grow up where we were lucky enough to grow up. An opportunity for us to become the stewards of these woodlands, and take some responsibility for what happens here."

I could tell Marley had practiced that speech for a while, but it hit some notes that resonated in me, especially that last part about responsibility. The Children of the Wheel did what they did with or without us witnessing it, but maybe some of my repressed guilt would be assuaged by being more present; investing myself into under-standing the whats and whys of the Wheel. I could do that if I lived closer. Plus Claudia really was sick of the city, and the conversation about moving north was coming up more and more as the years progressed.

"Mom and Dad need to go somewhere nice. That part needs to happen whether or not we decide we're doing this. They need—"

I didn't even get to finish my sentence before Marley reached into his pocket, and showed me what he already had keyed up on his phone's screen. It was a gorgeous, senior-friendly home in Ft. Laud-erdale. He really had thought of everything.

"It's literally the best retirement community on the planet. They will want for nothing."

I rubbed my temples as I came to a decision. I'd been unconsciously stress-clenching my jaw for so long I was starting to develop a headache.

"Swimming pool."

"Yeah man, it's right here in the pictures."

"No. *I* want a swimming pool. A nice in-ground one. You know I always wanted a pool in that backyard when I was a kid. Quinn and Dee-Dee would love it. And I don't want to buy it. I want *you* to buy it."

"You and your fucking pools. I do remember that. I know you have the money, but fuck it. What's another hundred grand at this point."

We stood regarding each other in the middle of the street, our frozen breath billowing into the night air like twin locomotive exhausts.

"Now what do we do?" Marley asked.

"All of this is gonna hinge on what Claudia says, but right this second? I guess we pop in and tell Mom and Dad they're finally moving to Florida."

CHAPTER
EIGHT

I thought it might be difficult to explain things to my parents, but as it turns out, having a billionaire best friend who famously spent money like it had an expiration date did most of the persuasive heavy lifting for me. They were over-the-moon excited about the house in Florida. My mom wrapped Marley in a weepy bear hug, and my dad gave him the most vigorous handshake I'd ever seen him offer anyone in my life. We celebrated at my old kitchen table with a dusty bottle of Champagne Dad had hidden in the laundry room for some special occasion. A week later, they were on a plane.

As Marley predicted, his parents didn't budge. Marley's dad, still as big of an asshole as ever, rejected every single offer Marley made them. A mansion in the French countryside. A luxury flat in Lisbon. A house right next to my parents in Florida. Fifty million dollars to do whatever they wanted with. Marley's dad scoffed at all of it, and said he couldn't be bought with his "playboy son's funny money." Marley had seen that coming from a mile away, and had already begun extravagant renovations on Mr. Grimford's Tudor-style house, which he'd always said was his favorite on the entire street.

I flew home and told Claudia what Marley had done, obviously minus the parts about the Wheel. She'd never been a fan of Marley's, but that wasn't enough to overpower her long-held desire to have the kids spend their formative years in a slower paced rural setting. We put our apartment on the market, got the kids registered at their new school, and we were living in my childhood home within a month.

One night after we were all settled in, Claudia washed a sink full of dinner dishes as I got ready to go over to Marley's house.

"Oh, I forgot it was poker night."

I could sense a tinge of disappointment in her voice.

Being an adult with a wife and children created certain logistical hurdles for me when it came to the Wheel. Sneaking out in the middle of the night gets quite a bit more difficult when you're sleeping next to someone. Of course, Marley was prepared for this as well. He'd decided he'd "host a bimonthly poker game for us and some old friends from school" Having to deceive my family about the Wheel had always been something that weighed on me, but the poker game afforded us plenty of time to hike out to the Wheel. Marley was always better at cover stories than I was.

"Yeah", I lied. "Marley has it in for me tonight. Remind me to never win against him again. He won't rest until he takes the pot back from me."

"Well, you could always stay home." Claudia said, resting a clean pot on the drying rack. "The girls are sleeping. We could watch a movie, crack a bottle of wine…"

"That actually sounds like a perfect night, doesn't it."

"It does. Maybe you can call Marley and cancel?"

I locked eyes with Claudia. Her face dropped the way it always did when I sacrificed our time together for Marley. It killed me to let her down like that, but I had no choice. Me going to the Wheel is what kept everything glued together at home. I had to continue lying, despite how bad I felt I was at it.

"I'm sorry, babe. I know, I know. But I already promised him, and you know how he's going to get if I turn him down at the last minute. Maybe I can skip the next game."

Claudia sighed, and resumed loading the dishwasher.

"Try not to be too late, I guess."

"Babe."

"No, I'm being weird. You go and have fun. It's OK."

It was not OK, but I left anyway.

By the time I walked over to Marley's place, he was already locking his side door. I met him on the side lawn, and we walked over to the woodlands gate together. I noticed the high-end hiking boots he wore on our excursions to the Wheel were caked in fresh mud.

"Didn't take you for a landscaping kind of guy."

"Huh?"

"Your boots. Looks like you just finished one of those Spartan races."

Marley looked down and almost seemed surprised by what he saw. "Oh! That! Yeah, just some mucking about in the yard. You know how it goes. You ready to head out?"

"Yeah, sorry I'm a little late. Claudia wasn't thrilled about me coming over tonight."

Marley chuckled. "Fucking women. She's sucking your energy dry, my man."

By Marley's design, the only way through his heavily fortified perimeter fence around was in his backyard. It required a code that changed daily, which only he had access to. As he keyed it in, a claustrophobic pang settled into my chest. Marley loved to talk about how we had a partnership, but he was the one controlling everything. We, including my family who had no idea why we were really there, all lived inside Marley's razor-wired cage.

The lock buzzed, and the gate swung open.

"Alright", Marley said. "Let's hit the gas station for a fill-up."

CHAPTER
NINE

I remember when the first kid went missing. We'd just celebrated our third anniversary of moving back to the old neighborhood. I was sitting on the couch watching a live CNN interview in which an unhinged Marley screamed "I'm a billionaire, I could set a nursing home on fire and not get arrested" when I received an Amber Alert text about a twelve-year-old boy from a few towns away not having come home from school. New Hampshire was one of the safest states in the country, but even we had the occasional missing child story. Claudia and I talked about how horrible it was, and hoped they found him soon. And that was it.

About a month later, the local sheriff's department held a press release about how the state's missing child averages were slightly up that year, and warned parents to keep an eye out for anything suspicious going around the home. Inappropriate contact with strangers, that kind of thing. Of course, that was concerning for a parent to hear, but I almost laughed out loud. Sure, I'll get right on setting up a neighborhood watch for our cul-de-sac in the woods that had been nearly empty for years.

When one of Quinn's classmates went missing two months after that, Claudia and I started getting nervous. We were luckier than most, as our kids were bussed to and from school, and were supervised by adults the entire time, but still. We decided at least one of us would hang out with the kids at the bus stop before and after school until things calmed down. I'd started retrofitting our house with an elaborate security system. Window sensors, motion detection, cameras, the works. At first Claudia and I fought about it because she thought it was paranoid and unnecessary, but as time went on and none of the missing children had been found, she came around to the idea.

When I finished installing our security system at the house, it came to mind that Marley already had his place wired up like one of those supermax prisons, and he had cameras all over his property. I walked over shortly after and asked him if we could take a look at his security footage just in case there was a glimpse of a missing kid or anything strange on them. I was a little worried he'd think I was somehow accusing him of something by asking that, so I was taken aback when he immediately handed me a stack of CD-ROMs with dates and times written on them in black Sharpie.

"Oh yeah, I made these for you a couple ago. I already scoured through all the footage and I didn't find anything, but I figured it didn't hurt to have a second set of eyes on it. Like you said, just in case."

I thanked Marley for thinking of me, and spent a few weeks going over every inch of those recordings on my office computer, but I never spotted anything outside of the occasional deer or hedgehog.

I was mowing the lawn when the local police showed up at Marley's house a few days after that, asking for Marley to let them through the gate so they could have a search party comb the woodlands for the little boy. It was inevitable, I knew. We owned a massive patch of land and they were running out of areas to look for that boy. I recognized one of the officers as the one tasked with organizing the search efforts in town, something Claudia and I had helped with a couple times, so I walked over to watch Marley at work. I remember briefly noticing his long-sleeved shirt and jeans and wondering why he was so bundled up on a hot summer day, but good luck getting Marley to explain any decision at any given moment.

"Totally appreciate what you guys are doing, but the kid isn't in there." Manipulating a couple small town cops out into believing searching the property was a fool's errand—or even convincing them that they'd already completed the search and found nothing—would be like opening a can of soda for Marley. Effortless, more of a subconscious act than anything. He could have probably ripped a fart and had those two barking like dogs or making out with each other. "Those woods are locked up like Fort Knox. A Navy Seal couldn't get in there, let alone a little kid."

"We can definitely appreciate the level of security you have surrounding this property, sir, but we really do have to be thorough. I'm sure you understand."

I braced myself for Marley's push.

"You know what?" Marley offered the two cops a wide, white smile. "You're right. A kid's life is on the line. Gotta check everywhere."

I laughed. I couldn't help myself. It was so absurdly fucking stupid. Marley had spent more money on securing that patch of woods than most people see after having worked their entire lives...and he was just going to let them in?

The two cops looked at me as if I'd just shit myself. I stopped laughing and turned to Marley.

"Marley, what the hell?"

Marley threw his hands up in that classic *I surrender* gesture. "No games here, neighbor. Just trying to be accommodating for the law. What do you guys think? Get everyone over here tomorrow morning and I'll unlock the gate?"

They agreed and drove away shortly after, but not before offering me the deranged neighbor who laughs at efforts to located a missing child a baffled look. Marley was smiling so hard I almost thought the top of his head was going to roll off onto his perfectly manicured lawn. It was the same smile he offered when we were in college and he'd figured out how to use a black box to get free cable with all the expensive movie channels in his dorm room, or when he'd score free food by walking into a fast-food restaurant and telling them they'd forgotten a cheeseburger in the drive-thru order he hadn't placed. It was his "I'm successfully gaming a system because I'm smarter than everyone around me" smile.

"Alright, they're gone. Mind explaining what the hell you're doing?"

"Relax, Caleb. It'll be fine. We'll let them stomp around a bit and they'll leave when they don't find anything."

"Don't find anything?! Marley, you spent millions securing the woods to keep civilians out because it's dangerous for them in there. What if they stumble across Old Friend? Why would you even risk it? Why wouldn't you just use your power to redirect their focus? And why am I not being looped in on these decisions?"

"Oh, I'm sorry. I didn't realize you split the bill on this thing with me and that this was a democracy."

"Oh no no, *I'm* sorry, Marley. I didn't realize this wasn't a democracy because you insisted this *was* a democracy when you convinced me to move back here. I didn't sign up to be under the thumb of an asshole dictator, and I sure as shit didn't sign up knowing you would eventually endanger innocent lives because you felt like gambling. If that's how you want to play it I'll pack the family up and head back to the city."

"Dude, chill. It's going to be fine. They won't find anything in there. Not if they search during the day."

"How could you possibly know that? We've never tried finding it during the day."

There was the briefest of pauses, and then Marley said "Listen, I could have used my powers, but I think we can both agree we could use a little appreciation from the community. Look what we did here. We privatized and blockaded a massive chunk of land, Caleb. Houses they could have bought and lived in. Woodlands they used to traipse through whenever they wanted. People talk. I'm sure you've experienced some off-putting looks from locals at PTA meetings and the grocery store. Sure, most of them know us from growing up and it's not like we're a pair of out-of-staters sucking up the town's resources, but they're not exactly thrilled with us these days."

My rage ebbed just enough for Marley's logic to sink in. I'd never put two and two together until that moment. I was never gifted with being able to read people, but Claudia mentioned weird vibes she'd picked up on from parents at school. Even from the guy working the register at the Yankee Deli up the road had said something like "Extra mustard? Anything for the *King of the Woods.*" I'd assumed it was just general tension from all of the missing children news, but examining it all through Marley's lens I could see it more clearly. We did need to make some kind of gesture, but why not a block party or some kind of fundraiser? Why did it have to be something that came with so much risk?

"And before you even ask, I was always gonna go in there with them. You can come too if you're not busy, but it's Saturday morning and I'm sure you have to watch the kids at home. If anything gets squirrely in there, I'll just nudge them back through the gate and that'll be that."

I walked back home and finished mowing the lawn just in time for Claudia to tell me dinner was ready. She'd made tacos, the cheap kind from a boxed kit. I know they're not *real* tacos but I ate them a lot as a kid and still have a weirdly nostalgic love of them. I washed up and sat at the table in a daze, still trying to process what had transpired at Marley's. I was halfway through my first taco before I realized Claudia, Quinn, and Dee-Dee were all staring at me, smiling.

"Okay" I said. "What's going on here?"

Dee-Dee giggled and clasped her hands over her mouth.

"What do you think of the tacos?" Claudia asked.

I squinted at her, trying to puzzle out what kind of game they were playing. "They're great! You did a great job with them, as always."

At that Quinn burst out laughing, spilling a mouthful of half-chewed taco back onto her plate.

"Well that's great" Claudia said, smiling that million-dollar smile of hers, "but I didn't make these tacos."

I looked at Dee-Dee and Quinn. Both of them were beaming with pride. "Wait, you're telling me—"

"WE MADE THE TACOS, DADDY!"

It was Claudia's turn to laugh. "Surprise!"

"That's right, Daddy! Me and Quinn cut up the vegetables and grated the cheese and cooked the ground beef and *everything!*"

"They were very very careful with the knives and stove. I was *very* impressed with our little chefs. And what do we say about the knives and stove, kids?"

"NEVER USE THEM WHEN MOM AND DAD AREN'T HOME!"

I remember saying "Wow!" and "That's amazing, girls!" and "I'm so proud of you two!", but guilt was pulping me from the inside out. It was a huge milestone moment for my daughters and I'd missed it because I was with Marley. I'd been with Marley when Dee-Dee first rode her bike without training wheels, and again when Quinn won the school spelling bee. I realized then I was missing so much of theirs and Claudia's lives because of my preoccupation with my best friend, the Wheel, maintaining a lifetime worth of secrets; all of it. Of course I couldn't admit this to anyone at the table. I just laughed and blotted my eyes with the corner of my napkin, and ate my amazing daughters' tacos.

I did join the search party the following morning, much to Marley's dismay. I would have stayed home to make pancakes for the kids if I actually trusted Marley to do the right thing out there, but letting him go alone didn't sit right in my gut. I needed to make sure he didn't do something stupid. He resented me feeling like he couldn't do it on his own, but what was I if not Marley's lifelong babysitter?

We spent the entire day combing the woodlands with over a hundred people from town; a long horizontal line of us stretching from one fenced in boundary to the other. We picked through the scrub brush and detritus looking for signs of the little boy; a tennis shoe, the lunchbox he'd gone to school with that day, anything. I spent most of the time nervously scanning the hills for signs of the Wheel, or what I imagined would be a very angry Old Friend had he seen the crowd we'd invited without permission. I noticed very early on that my internal compass wasn't pulling me in any particular direction, which was the only thing was keeping me from experiencing a full-blown panic attack.

We all funneled back through the gate at dusk. We'd found no trace of the boy, or the Wheel, or Old Friend, or anything other than mosquito bites and a few thorn-scraped legs. Everyone thanked us for letting them search the property and dispersed. When they were gone, Marley gave me an insufferable look I knew all too well. *I told you so.*

"Okay" I said, "That smug piece of shit look on your face needs to disappear right now."

"Why are you harshing my high, man? I feel like I just hit it big at the casino!"

I could feel myself grinding my teeth in frustration. It was like I was talking to someone who was experiencing an entirely different reality from mine. It was often like that with Marley.

"Yes. Congratulations. Your little stunt played out like you knew it would, but maybe we save the confetti and Champagne for an actual win."

"What are you even talking about?"

"Marley. Local kids are going missing, and there's a Wheel in the woods that chews up kids. We barely understand the thing, and we're not watching it 24/7. You're telling me you've never speculated that the two are somehow connected?"

Marley's smile continued to grow. He was basking in my anger. "You really haven't thought this through, have you? I have this place locked up like a military base. Second, you're the god damned compass, Caleb. Nobody can find the Wheel without you. If I didn't know you like I do and I was certain the Wheel had something to do with it, I'd have to wonder if *you* were somehow involved with the disappearing kiddos."

I wanted to slug him in the face. It was the most absurd Marley-esque table-turning argumental switcheroo. He'd managed to neatly shut down any and all speculation about the Wheel and his ironclad rationalizations while simultaneously patronizing me, and I couldn't bring myself to debate it because it actually made sense. It didn't satisfy the nagging feeling that had been keeping me awake at night ever since that first kid went missing, but feelings weren't evidence. Feelings weren't the currency with which I could buy Marley's attention.

"My god, you are such an asshole."

"You're right, I'm an asshole. But I'm a *correct* asshole and you know it. Dude, breathe. Don't sweat it. Your kids are safe. At this point your house has more security systems on it than mine, and they're gonna find whoever's doing this shit sooner than later. Every cop in the state is on this. They're gonna catch some crazed hobo or unhinged junkie drywaller trying to lure a kid into a panel van with a bag of gummy bears, and that'll be that. Trust me."

I sighed. "Fine. Alright. You're right."

"Hey, why don't you come in for a beer or seven? We've been at it all day, and Mom's in the kitchen making whoopee pies from scratch."

I WAS PAYING invoices in my home office when I got a call from Claudia.

"I'm at the school. Quinn got into a fistfight with a classmate and is suspended for a week. Everything will be fine, but I just want to give you a heads up before we head home."

I remember saying "What?" several times, as if Claudia's words were bouncing off my confused brain. Quinn wasn't an angry kid, definitely not a schoolyard brawler. She was as agreeable as they came, and had a ton of friends. Her teachers loved her. Her grades were reasonable. Before that day she'd never gotten so much as a detention.

A red-faced Quinn hopped out and slammed the car door shut before Claudia had a chance to put it in park. I made it five steps to the front door before it flew open.

"Alright, what happened, Quinnie?"

Instead of answering me, she stormed up the stairs and slammed her bedroom shut. Claudia came in a moment later.

"What the hell is going on, babe?"

Claudia dumped her purse on the table by the door where we kept all of our mail and keys and sighed. "Apparently Angel said something mean to her in the hallway. It escalated, and teachers pulled them off each other."

Again, I was gob smacked. Angel was Quinn's best friend. They never argued. She had sleepovers here just about every other weekend.

"What did Angel say?"

Claudia didn't answer. She was struggling with opening a bottle of wine. It wasn't even eleven in the morning. My dread was compounding by the second.

"Babe, what did Angel say to Quinnie to make a fight break out?"

"They were making a diorama about notable local residents for their history class, and Angel said she shouldn't be allowed to participate because…"

Claudia trailed off as she filled a glass to the top with Chardonnay. By that point I was starting to get upset with her making me feel like I had to pry the information out her.

"Because why, Claudia?"

"Because she's not really from here. Because her family bought up a big chunk of town and won't let anyone use it. Because…"

"Claudia, Jesus Christ. Out with it."

"Because the kids in her class started a rumor a while back about the missing children are somewhere behind our fence. They're saying we have something to do with it."

"That's fucking ridiculous."

"That's what your daughter said. A lot of this I heard second-hand from the principal when I was called in, but apparently Quinn said the police and half the town were in there looking and didn't find anything."

"Well what did Angel have to say about that?"

"She said that didn't mean anything, that if we had enough money to buy all this land then we have enough money to buy off some cops. They're kids, Caleb. They're not gonna let logic get in the way of the rumor mill. Things escalated, they got into a shoving match, and Quinn broke Angel's nose."

"Oh. Well. Fuck."

Claudia took a long sip from her glass and held it up in a mock toast. "Yes. Fuck."

"I'm going to go upstairs and talk with her."

"Honey, just give her some time to cool down first. She's really upset."

"I just wish she'd said something to us before letting it boil over. We could have done something. Parent-teacher conference. *Something.*"

At that, Claudia put her wineglass down so hard I thought it was going to shatter.

"She did say something, Caleb. I've been dealing with this for weeks."

I remember staring back at my wife, a deep hurt creeping into my heart as long withheld words tumbled out of her like crab apples from a spilled basket. They'd been keeping things from me. Claudia. The kids. My family. The most important people in my life who I'd thought were open and honest about everything.

"What? Why didn't anyone tell me?" I was already moving toward the staircase despite Claudia warning me to give Quinn some space. I didn't care about what she wanted at that point. I was angry. I felt betrayed. I wanted some answers.

"Because you're obsessed with this insane idea, Caleb. Us living in your childhood neighborhood; your childhood home. Nobody around us but your shitty best friend who duped you into thinking this would be a good thing. No other adults for us to have dinner with. No kids for Quinnie and Dee-Dee to play with. It's just us in this eerie, empty space that has everyone else in town hating our guts, and none of us feel like we can talk to you about how much this place creeps us out because you want it so badly all the signs of this not being great are just bouncing off of you."

At that point I tuned Claudia out. Not my proudest moment, but everything she was saying was too much for me to take in all at once, so instead of listening to her like a reasonable husband, I stormed up the stairs to Quinn's room. I remember feeling like I just needed to fix something; anything. Knowing I made one thing a little bit better that day would have given me a foothold of confidence that would provide enough emotional stability to weather the rest of it.

I rapped on her bedroom door a few times. "Quinnie? It's Dad. Can we talk?"

She didn't answer. My frustration was building. Quinn *always* answered when I called for her. Both my daughters did. My perception of my family was sifting through my fingers like sand. I tried the door-knob. It was locked.

My frustration was building to a thin dread. Something was wrong.

"Quinnie? Open up please. This isn't funny. I want to talk with you about what happened today, okay?"

Again, no answer came.

I walked to the linen closet in the upstairs hallway, where we kept the small metal prods used to poke the doorknob locks open. I grabbed one and fumbled it into the knob with shaking fingers. The lock mechanism sprung open with a small metallic pop.

"Honey, I'm opening the door. I don't know what's gotten into you, but—"

I stopped mid-sentence as I realized I was speaking to an empty room. Her school backpack had been thrown to the ground in front of her bedroom window, which was wide open.

She was gone.

CLAUDIA and I walked up and down the deserted cul-de-sac screaming Quinn's name for hours. When we weren't yelling, we were peeking in through the windows of the empty houses to see if she was hiding in any of them.

When we weren't doing that, we were yelling at each other. The stress of having a daughter run away as local children were going missing all over the place made it all tumble out, and I remember feeling confused because I had no idea either of us were harboring any of it. Resentments about our individual parenting styles. Our having respectively failed each other as friends and spouses and parents. The decision to pry the kids out of the lives they knew in the city. We argued. We blamed each other. I refused to find any merit in what Claudia said, and insisted the situation at school would blow over in time, as would the disdain of the adults in town.

Everything is awkward at first, I remember yelling as we screamed for Quinn. Everything is awkward until it isn't. *Just give it time.* I briefly wished I had some of Marley's power, a little woods magic to help her understand how good they had it; anything to keep me from having to explain the truth about why we were there.

I was just about to call the police when I heard a door shutting in the near distance. I turned to Marley's house, and saw Quinn bounding down his driveway with an ice cream cone in one hand, undoubtedly from the soft serve machine Marley had installed in his kitchen a few months earlier. Claudia and I let out a collective sigh, and I could feel the tension drain from my back and shoulders. She was okay.

"What the fuck was she doing over there?"

Claudia had her hands on her hips as the relief gave way to the rage of a frustrated wife and mother. "Apparently Uncle Marley told the girls they can come over if there's ever trouble at the house."

Marley appeared in the doorway shortly after, and offered us a conciliatory wave. Claudia was instantly on him like a pit bull.

"Don't you ever do that again, you son of a bitch. Your house isn't a place for my children to hide from their responsibilities and punishments. That is wildly inappropriate. *We* are her parents. *You* are her neighbor. You want to play Daddy? Have your own fucking kids."

Marley laughed the laugh of someone who was forever faultless, and held his hands up in the air as if he were being arrested at gunpoint.

"Easy, tiger! She came knocking on my door all upset. What did you want me to do? Let her wander? Last I checked kids are going missing left and right around here."

"What did I want you to do, Marley? I wanted you to call us. We've been worried sick running up and down the street for hours, and don't tell me you didn't hear us out here."

I didn't know what to say, so I said nothing. It was an overstep of a boundary. Several boundaries really, but it was a very aloof and very *Marley* overstep, and I was so used to protecting him from the consequences of those that I found myself wanting to calm my wife instead of joining her in her fury.

Neither of us could tear our eyes away from our daughter who would soon be extremely grounded for a month, a silent pact lingering between us. *This particular discussion is tabled for now, but it's not even close to being over.*

⊗

"I DID IT! They finally moved out!"

Marley was nearly doing a jig in his driveway as I walked up it. It was another ritual night, and I'd brought a platter of chicken parmesan I'd whipped up for us. Even as a billionaire, Marley never had food in his fridge. He always said it was because he was too busy to have groceries delivered, but his mom was right next door to stock his shelves whenever he wanted. I knew it was part of his self-image obsession that had mutated into body dysmorphia. Having snacks in the house meant pumping calories into the sculpted body that helped him feel like he was better than everyone else. I'd also noticed a small mountain of over-the-counter stomach medication in his bathroom the last time I was over. All that booze on an empty stomach was causing problems even the boon couldn't fix, I guessed.

Marley hadn't been looking good lately. He had dark circles under his eyes and he'd lost some weight, which he'd attributed to some business dealings that had kept him up late. I figured a home cooked meal and some company might do him some good.

"Dad's doctor has been insisting he move to a warmer climate forever. Something about it being better for his fragile old man health. He finally caved. Let me buy him and Mom a nice little desert cottage in Sedona. Shit, if I knew that's all it would take, I would have paid his doctor to tell him that ages ago."

"Jesus", I said. "Only took half your life to finally convince them. When did this happen? Your parents never mentioned anything about moving, not that I talk to them a lot. I don't even remember seeing a truck out front."

"Four days ago! I think you and Claudia were at one of the kids' soccer tournaments or something. My secretary hired a white-glove moving service to handle it all for them. Mom and Dad didn't have to lift a finger. In and out in five hours."

I was happy for him, in a weird way. Whether it was college or living in New York, Marley always did better when the specter of his emotionally abusive father wasn't looming over him. Even in his dotage, that miserable old prick knew just what screw to twist in order to pitch Marley into abject outrage. Marley's mother was constantly over at his place to cook and clean, but in the years we'd been back at the cul-de-sac, Marley might have visited his father at the house he grew up in only three or four times. I didn't blame him. I was sure he'd at least miss his mother, but sometimes making a clean break from toxic people also means creating space between you and the people who enable them.

I had originally wanted to talk with him regarding the ongoing search for the missing children, and whether or not we should be concerned about how strange the Wheel had been acting. How the wobble had gotten far worse, and how the dark, mottled splotches on it had given way to an unsettling pinkish-purple translucence. I wanted to ask him if he thought it would be a good idea to maybe ask the Children what was going on before the ritual, but it had been so long since I'd seen Marley that happy. I didn't want to spoil it.

The next morning after the ritual, I heard the diesel roar of heavy construction equipment. I looked through the window. Marley had rented a bulldozer and a skid steer loader, and was personally demolishing his childhood home. He was very drunk. I watched him for hours. Occasionally he'd let loose a triumphant scream as walls collapsed, and windows shattered. He didn't stop until the sun set, and the craftsman-style prison in which a set of parents failed their son had been reduced to splintered lumber and dusty drywall chunks.

Marley went missing five days later.

CHAPTER
TEN

It was his driver Richard who first let us know Marley wasn't around. He knocked on our door after waiting for Marley in his driveway for thirty minutes, and asked if we knew where he might be. He wasn't answering phone calls or texts either. I told his Richard not to worry. We all knew how impulsive The Rasputin of Wall Street could be. He was probably on a remote tropical island with no internet, love bombing some young actress for a couple weeks. Richard agreed, and asked that I tell Marley to call him whenever he gets home.

I didn't start worrying until another five days of Marley not bothering to answer phone calls, texts, or even emails. Even if he was trying to enjoy an unplugged vacation, there's no way he would've gone an entire week without checking in. Something felt off. Of course, I was concerned about his well-being, but the next ritual was also only four days away. If he wasn't back by then, both of us would be in big trouble. Marley had the only access code to the gate leading in and out of the woodlands, and he'd had that fence engineered so well even a team of Blackwater operatives couldn't scale it without casualties. Marley had convinced me to move back home, and resume our regular visits to the Wheel, and because of that, I was fully dependent on that boon. If Marley stayed gone, both of our boons would be gone. Our careers, our money our health, my wife, my kids, my everything. Gone.

Fucking Marley.

CHAPTER
ELEVEN

Two days later, I was making breakfast for the girls in the kitchen before school. Dee-Dee busied herself by dribbling spoonfuls of cereal on the front of her Adventure Time sweatshirt, while her older sister Quinn ignored her toast in favor of a crayon drawing she was doodling at the table. It was a picture of our house, with a black and brown scribble on the side of it that reminded me of Pig Pen's dirt cloud.

"What's this, honey?"

"That's the thing that sometimes tries to wake me up at night."

"Oh wow, that looks scary. Did you have a bad dream?"

"I don't know. Maybe? I heard something hitting the window in my bedroom. It woke me up. When I got out of bed to see what it was, there was something down there. It was waving for me to come outside. It happens every now and then."

My stomach dropped as a core memory from childhood trickled into my brain, and choked out all other thought. I jogged to my office computer to check the security camera footage, but remembered a falling branch had taken that one out and I was still waiting for a replacement, so that side of the house was currently unmonitored. I walked outside, and around to the side of the house where Quinn's bedroom window was on the second floor. I scoured the grass on that side of the lawn, as well as the mulch beds and hardscaping.

It didn't take long to find the shiny copper BBs glinting in the early morning sunlight.

CHAPTER
TWELVE

I couldn't call the police. That's what I remember thinking after the girls had gone to school, as I stood in the kitchen holding my fourth mug of coffee, staring at the tiles on the floor. I couldn't tell my wife because she'd think I was crazy, and I couldn't call the police because they'd think I was crazy. They'd also probably get a warrant to search Marley's house, and maybe even crack their way through the perimeter fence. God only knew what would happen if they started traipsing through the woodlands on a manhunt. I was powerless to do anything but let the sinking feeling in my chest continue bearing down on me.

Making matters worse, the next ritual was supposed to take place later that night. If Marley didn't come home in time, I didn't have the access code for the gate. My best friend disappeared off the face of the earth, and I was in genuine danger of losing everything I cared about in life. Part of me felt guilty for thinking about myself while Marley could be in very real danger, or worse.

I glanced outside, and my coffee mug slid out of my hands, shattering on the floor.

The Children of the Wheel were standing in my backyard, staring at me through the window.

I felt hot coffee seep into my socks as eleven smiling children waited patiently for me to notice them. Morning sun reflected brightly off their white nightgowns and pale skin. They shaded their eyes with their hands, seemingly unconditioned to so much light. Anxiety gripped my chest. Our trips to visit them were always one-way. Never before had they left the woods. I didn't even know they were able to until that moment.

One of them motioned for me to come outside to them, and very hesitantly, I obliged.

"You...you can come here?" I remember feeling like an idiot after asking this. Obviously, they could go there, because there they were.

"You need to come to the hill," they sang in unison.

"What, like now? It's not time yet."

"Precisely. Please follow us."

One of the children held my hand as we reached the electrified perimeter fence, and I flinched as we walked right through it as if it were nothing but mist.

There was still so much I didn't know about the children.

They led me through the woodlands to the rocky hill, which was still bathed in alien moonlight. The whirling Wheel hung as it always did, inches off the ground. Only the Wheel had changed dramatically since Caleb had seen it only a couple of weeks earlier. The pinkish-purple translucence had completely taken over the pale granite, and its shockingly violent wobble reminded me of a rim fighting to stay on a speeding car after the driver forgot to tighten the lug nuts. Its grinding side didn't look as scrubbed clean as it normally did. A brownish-red streak coated it.

It looked unstable. It looked *wrong*.

When we reached the top of the hill, the Children of the Wheel asked me to sit down, another first in our interactions with them. I did as I was asked, and they all sat in a circle around me.

And then they proceeded to sing about me why they'd summoned me.

"WE'VE BEEN WATCHING the sly one for years, at first intrigued by his experiments," they started, and immediately the hair on the nape of my neck stood on end. I tried to figure out how Marley could have gotten to the Wheel without me and my compass, but what the fuck did I expect? It's Marley. Even before the Wheel's boon he'd once concocted a scheme to get free Taco Bell by convincing frazzled drive-thru attendants they'd forgotten a few items in his order. Of course he figured out a way to bypass me.

"At first, his attempts to talk to Old Friend were amusing, but he got better. He used his powers of manipulation on Old Friend, insisting Demelae would be pleased by his work. Old Friend allowed the sly one to feed different things into the Wheel to see what happened. He started with rats and birds. Demelae's domain never opened up for those offerings, which merely flew in ragged clumps to the grass on the other side of the Wheel. This made Old Friend hesitant to continue allowing the experimentation. The sly one applied his gift of persuasion on Old Friend, but discovered the limit of it when he attempted feeding one of us into the Wheel unwillingly. They kicked and writhed in the sly one's grip. Old Friend put a stop to that quickly, and directed the sly one to leave."

I couldn't believe what I was hearing, but as I listened, a familiar trickle of icy panic began dripping down the back of my spine, and pooled in my stomach. It was the feeling I always got when someone tried telling me they'd been hurt by Marley. It was my body physically rejecting truth in favor of the, what, exactly? Marley's preferred version of events? Me choosing the path of least resistance to keep him from flipping out or ghosting me? Had I been *trained* to do that for all those years?

The Children of the Wheel continued to sing their story for me.

"We howled with rage as he dragged his first human sacrifice up the rocky hill to the Wheel. It was a without-home woman he'd found walking a set of 'train tracks'. Once again, the sly one manipulated Old Friend into standing aside. Demelae didn't accept this offering either. Instead, She sent it back into the center of the sly one's chest, where it was instantly absorbed. The newly exalted sly one gasped as Demelae's nourishment filled his body with power."

"Why didn't you tell me earlier?!" It was all I could manage to sputter out as the revelations filled my mind to overflowing. *The woods,* I thought stupidly. *That's how he knew nobody would find the Wheel during the day on that search for the missing children.*

"We assumed it was Master's will, that Old Friend would have intervened had our master not condoned the behavior of your friend.

He's fed innocents into the Wheel for years. Without-home people, perpetual travelers, sedation enthusiasts, and love contractors from far away. People he reasoned wouldn't be missed. His power grew by leaps and bounds. It was then that he led his parents to the hill."

"Finally had enough juice to bend your mean old dad to your will", I thought crazily, the full impact of Marley having murdered his own parents in the worst possible way still not having sunk all the way in.

"Through process of elimination, the sly one learned that children offered the purest level of power, and reasoned that it must be why Demelae preferred them. The sly one fed so many stray children into the Wheel that he became powerful enough to feed Old Friend into the Wheel. Old Friend howled in pain as his body was pulverized into dust that filled the sly one's eyes, nose, and mouth. The incredible surge of energy from ingesting Demelae's creation was too much for a human body to take in. It turned the sly one into something twisted and vile. Part man, and part something else we don't have words for."

When the Children of the Wheel got to that part of the story, I rolled over on my hands and knees, and vomited that morning's coffee into the grass. Too many puzzle pieces clicked together all at once. My mind reeled. That brownish black swirl of crayon in Quinn's drawing. The uptick in missing children across the state.

The BBs under my daughter's window.

I wretched into the grass again. When I was finished, I wiped my mouth on my sleeve, and looked at the children.

"Where is he?"

"He is currently stuck in our world, suffering greatly. He is stuck there until tonight's ritual, when he will attempt to feed you to the Wheel. He knows your boon is set to fade if you don't come. After you, he'll turn to us. He will then be strong enough to kill Demelae, and feed Her to himself. If he does that, there will be thousand-mile lines of people from both of our worlds being coaxed into the Wheel."

I STOOD on top of that hill, after having listened to the children's horrifying account of Marley's covert misdeeds, his plans to betray me, his attempt to lure my own child out into the woods, and I cried. I felt so goddamned stupid. My best friend was a monster, something far worse than Old Friend. He was more like the alien entity living beyond that shimmering black hole above the Wheel, the thing that manipulated innocent kids into believing it was an honor to be liquefied and consumed by it.

My lifelong best friend was no longer human; twisted by unknowable forces into something tortured and dangerous. But as I cried, and stared at the placid faces of the children, a sickening realization washed over me. Marley hadn't been human for a long, long time. At least not all the way human. His callousness, his indifference to the well-being of others, his obsessive, almost Machiavellian drive to manipulate and control the world around him. Marley was a severely troubled man. Had I come into contact with a stranger in possession of the same smorgasbord of easily identifiable narcissistic, psychopathic tendencies, I'd have known to run screaming. But I understood with a dawning clarity that I'd been carefully groomed by Marley to ignore his myriad red flags since I was just a boy, long before the Wheel supercharged our inherent natures. His survival hinged on making naïve people believe he was a fun, charming, successful guy, right up until he drained them dry, and decided they no longer held value for him. I was never his friend, not in any true sense of the word. I was never special to him. I was only useful. Marley was an opportunistic predator, and whether it happened in our teenage years, or in our forties on that rocky hill in another world, I was always destined to number among his victims.

"We have something in common, you and us." One of the children said as she reached to hold my hand, prying me out of my self-deprecating spiral. "It appears we've also been betrayed."

"What do you mean? By Marley?"

"The unforgivable crimes your friend committed here and the subsequent lack of response from Demelae has forced us to reconsider our position as Children of the Wheel. Like you, we have been trained to accept our roles from a very young age. Witnessing your friend's thirst for power and indifference to life of all forms has shaken us from our collective stupor, and has brought to light the very same callousness and indifference in our master. There was never anything holy here. Nothing sacred. Just an endless cycle of treachery and slaughter perpetrated against innocents."

I opened my mouth to speak, but then closed it again. *From a very young age?* Just how old *were* the Children of the Wheel?

"We understand the depth of your pain, Caleb, as I hope you understand ours. We cannot fathom the guilt you feel for having partaken in the Wheel's boon for so long, now knowing the true cost of it. But we do not have time to wallow. Tonight, in a handful of your hours, whether you stay in your home, or here on this hill, your friend comes for you. We've brought you here to edify you, as well as to discuss our plan of action. It will require great strength and sacrifice on all of our parts. The question becomes this: are you willing to do what it takes to stop all of this, Caleb? To prevent a life-eradicating cata-strophe that would span worlds? To end the tyranny of our Demelae, as well as *your* Demelae?"

The children drew my attention to a clump of sticks and brush between the trees.

"Demelae is already constructing a new Old Friend so She can once again receive our sacrifices. But that takes time. Until then, this may be our only chance. To give ourselves to a different cause."

I contemplated those words for a moment, allowing them to steep in my stewing shame and rage and regret. And then I sat back down on the grass, and listened.

CHAPTER
THIRTEEN

The woodlands were quieter than they'd ever been, as if the creatures that called it home from time immemorial, as well as the wind that ceaselessly rustled foliage and whistled around branches, all braced themselves for what was to come.

The only sound was the sickly warbling thrum of the abused Wheel.

And then, the crunching of feet through dead leaf crust, and the snapping of dried twigs under weight.

There, at the base of the hill, the thing that was once Marley, or more like Marley than ever before, trundled its way up the steep incline. Bright moonlight bathed over its horrifying body. Bone and branch wove painfully in and out of mottled flesh that hung from its bulk in bloody tatters that swayed with the effort of its six humanoid legs, struggling to pump in crab-like unison over rocky outcroppings and around brush thickets; a nightmare newborn giraffe struggling to gain control of its new faculties. Six arms protruded from its globular torso, all waving slowly in different directions. Some arms ended in various pincers and sharpened wooden claws, one in a heavy, bulbous mass of moose skull and vine.

Its head, a pulsing, disfigured mockery of humanity, boasted the twisted, sightless faces of three different people. Black, greasy fumes billowed from their mouths and noses, as if something inside the abomination smoldered, cooking its organs, and pitching it into shuddering fits of anguish. When it bellowed, it came out as a harmonized, pleasantly tuned pitch from all three chattering mouths simultaneously; a howl of torment masked as a confident, alluring croon.

Marley eventually reached the top of the rocky hill, and took a moment to compose itself. Its chest heaving, drawing in fresh air, and expelling tire fire smoke into the night sky of another world.

Eventually, Marley stood up straight, the height of its new body towering past even Old Friend, who reached the center hole of the Wheel when it wasn't hunched over.

Then, using three soothing, beautiful voices, it harmonized "You can come out, Caleb. I know you're there. I know…I guess I know a lot now."

With that, I emerged from behind the Wheel.

Marley took one look at me, and began coughing. Great gouts of mucus and orange sparks erupted from its mouths, cascading down the bulk of its mutated body, and padding into the grass below. I could see then that the two other anguished faces grafted to his head were those of the mother and father he'd fed into the Wheel. Forever fused to both his enabler and his torturer. Even after everything he'd done, and everything he still wanted to do, it was impossible not to feel a pang of empathy for him.

"How?" the abomination that was Marley sang into the air between us like the tinkling of precious piano keys. "How?"

"'How' as in 'How did I know what you were up to?' or 'How' as in 'How did I manage to do all of this?'"

I gestured at myself, dripping head to toe in the blood and gore of the twelve cherubic, nightgowned children I'd spent the last several hours grinding into the Wheel, drinking in the viscera and power meant for a celestial being until I'd become as strong as the hulking horror before me. What was left of the children had cooled to a tacky pulp on my skin, and sent waves of energy pulsing through my naked body.

"The Children of the Wheel made a house call, if you can believe it.

Filled me in on your extra-curricular activities. They were the ones who proposed all of this. Apparently, they realized Demelae wasn't all that. They'd rather erase themselves from existence than spend another second being victimized by a monster. Boy oh boy, do I know that feeling."

"Listen, you have it all wrong, Caleb. Those kids, they were full of shit. They orchestrated this entire thing. Miserable little fucks. They wanted us to distrust each other. Can you believe it? It was all that thing in the hole's plan; get us to fight, weaken us. Then it could feed us both into the Wheel. Look what they did to me just to frighten you. I bet they told you I'd hurt you. They told you that, and then they made me this, to make sure you'd believe it. And look at you. You completely fell for it. Some friend you are."

Listening to him vomit pathology in his trio of angelic voices was incredibly disarming, just as I knew it was designed to be. It hadn't been long, but he'd already started figuring out how to manipulate the knobs and sliders of the control board that housed his new powers. Had I not just imbued myself with the fortifying essence of the children, I would've undoubtedly fallen for it.

"But now we can team up, right? Let's kick this Demelae's ass. Here, help me figure out how to summon the black hole above the Wheel. I've got Old Friend's bits and pieces rattling around in me. I'm sure I can figure it out."

Marley skittered over to the Wheel, its many legs working in practiced symphony, making me wonder if it had really been winded making the climb up the hill, or if it was just a ploy to lower my defenses, and make me believe it had been weakened by his transformation.

"You're not dumb, Marley. You are many things, and most of them are fucking abhorrent, but dumb isn't one of them. There aren't any more Children of the Wheel left on this side tonight. The food truck has left the parking lot. No reason for Demelae to open that door. It's over. The rituals, the boons. All of it."

Marley feigned disinterest with what I was saying, his back turned to me as his appendages waved about him; some kind of reverent conjuring I couldn't understand.

"You're right. I'm not dumb. There are obviously more Children of the Wheel. Where did you think the new ones replacing the ones Old Friend ground up came from? That world—er, this world, has a ton of them. I saw them myself. They're already lined up to replace the ones who deserted their posts. Even a new Old Friend, although they'll probably call him New Friend now, right? Old Friend v2.0? Also, Demelae doesn't open the door. The Wheel opens the door."

As if responding to its melodic voices, the shimmering black hole opened up above the Wheel, just as it always had on ritual nights.

"See? I told you. Now we just need to figure out how to get through it to the other side. Here, help me figure this out. Maybe I can give you ten fingers, and lift you up there. Hell, I can give you thirty!"

Marley casually motioned for me to come closer with its many arms. Closer to the Wheel. I didn't budge.

"Come here, Caleb." This time its singing came with force behind it, the harmonic tones trying to break through my emotional ramparts, and tug my heart into submission.

I didn't budge.

"COME HERE, CALEB."

My feet dug furrows in the grass as my body was propelled several feet forward by Marley's enraged will. I repositioned myself, and halted my progress. God damn, he was strong. I screamed at him as we fought out battle of wills, hoping against hope that my building rage would fortify me against his impossible magnetism.

"You can't even be honest about what's happening here, can you. You're so conditioned to getting whatever you want that you don't even possess the fortitude the rest of us build up over the years to deal with relentless disappointment. Instead, you just lie. To yourself, to everyone around you. You flail like a fucking toddler at the merest hint of 'no' to protect yourself from injury. I'm sorry, Marley, but you're getting nothing but 'no' from here on out."

"You did it, too!" Marley's voices screamed so loudly the trees around us vibrated. "You think I'm such a monster, but you stood there and watched those kids gets killed for decades! You just killed twelve of them with your bare hands! I never did so many at once before. Who's emotionally dishonest now, huh? Who's the monster now?"

Salty tears cut paths through the caked blood on my face. "Do you know how remorseful I am about all of it? Sitting through those rituals? Allowing children to die so I could have a nice little life for myself? Forcing myself to go numb enough to end the lives of those wonderful, beautiful children in order to stop you? I'll never erase any of that from my head. There's no amount of booze or therapy or escapism that'll scrub me clean."

Marley's faces trained on me. "I've never given a fuck how you felt about anything."

"Ironic, huh? After all that bitching and moaning about your dad, you really did turn out just like him."

I didn't even see the bony club at the end of one of Marley's appendages swinging at me. I just felt it connect with my chest, and then I was sailing backwards off the top of the hill like a dropkicked dodgeball. My flight was stopped by the trunk of an old oak tree, which my body slid down to the forest floor. I'd broken some ribs, but I could already feel them knitting back together under my skin. I still didn't know the extent of my new powers, but I needed to be a quick study if I was going to survive that encounter with Marley.

Suddenly, the brightness of that otherworldly moon was eclipsed by a black blob. *The black crayon squiggle in Quinn's drawing* was all I had time to think before I was forced to roll to the side, narrowly evading being crushed by Marley's punishing girth.

I rose to my feet, missing a pincer jab to my face by a hair before backpedaling out of Marley's reach. I pulled a young tree out of the ground, and swung it at Marley's head, the root ball connecting with a satisfying thud. Three of it legs buckled under the creature, and it let loose a harmonic howl of pain and rage that made my eyes vibrate. I swung it again, only for its pincer arm to shear the tree in half. I dropped it and ran for the hill. I made it maybe fifty feet before something connected with the back of my head, spiraling me into unconsciousness.

When I came to, I was being dragged up the hill, Marley's sharp clawed hand vice gripped around my exposed ankle.

"Like you were ever going to beat me in a fight. Get real, Caleb." It laughed as I tried prying its wooden fingers open, and grabbing at saplings to halt our slow, relentless progress toward the corrupted Wheel. I was powerless to do anything but watch myself being dragged toward a gruesome death. I was no match for Marley. All of those children, gone for nothing.

At the top, it picked me up by my head, and brought me in for a long hug; a mockery of Old Friend's ritualistic display of love and affection before the feedings began. I was unable to do anything but cringe. Its flesh was clammy and fevery hot, and smelled of old smoke, like an old campfire pit.

When it was done, it held me out in front of it like a rag doll, its head cocking slightly to the side like a puppy seeing its reflection in the mirror for the first time. Behind its bulk only five paces away, the edge of the Wheel wobbled and thrummed, blindly preparing itself to be of service to the lord beyond the schism above despite its terminal failings.

"We had a good run, you and I." Marley said, each of its faces grinning menacingly. "But I'm destined for greater things, and ever since we were kids, you've done nothing but hold me back. You had all the power in the world, and all you care about is your ugly family and your dumbshit paintings."

I slid my right hand into the pocket of my jeans. Slowly, as to not draw Marley's attention away from his self-congratulation.

Unsatisfied with my lack of response, Marley continued. "You know what? Honesty *does* feel pretty good. You're a fucking loser, Caleb. I was always the best part about your miserable life. At least you can go out knowing that."

My right arm pistoned out with unnatural speed and strength, releasing the handful of BBs I'd collected from the lawn earlier like a blast of birdshot. The tiny copper balls sunk deeply into Marley's faces, bursting his many eyes like rotten grapes.

It dropped me to the ground, clutching its faces with its two wooden clawed hands and howling beautifully. Its remaining appendages flailed out in every direction as he unknowingly stumbled closer to the Wheel. The bone club of one arm made a whining noise as it grazed the grinding edge, sending shards of skull and wood up into the black hole Marley had forgotten to close before the confrontation, which shivered with what I can only explain as its displeasure with the offering being presented through it.

Knowing I only had seconds to act before his eyes regenerated, I pulled another tree out of the ground, and rushed at Marley with it like a battering ram. Its entire body slammed into the spinning Wheel all at once, instantly coating the grinding edge with blood and muscle tissue. The Wheel bucked on its invisible axis, the bulk of Marley's monstrous body overloading its ability to safely convert human meat into sustenance for Demelae.

The thing that was once my best friend jittered and spasmed and shrieked as its body was consumed and fired up into the quivering black hole, from which a sound like a thousand babies screaming in unison came. I kept that tree pressed into Marley until his legs and arms dropped away, nothing left of the torso they'd once been attached to, and the end of my tree burst into flames from the friction.

I backed away from the Wheel as its gyrations became more and more erratic and unstable, and then everything went white.

CHAPTER
FOURTEEN

When I woke up, I was lying face down in a bush. After blinking the stars out of my eyes, I stood up and patted myself down, checking for injuries. High above, the beautiful, confounding multicolored alien nightscape of the other world gleamed and shimmered. I became frantic as I realized where I was, even more so when I scanned my immediate surroundings for the opening between worlds and found nothing. The Wheel was gone, and with it my ticket back home.

The top of the hill had been sheared off in the explosion. Trees all around me had been shattered, only the trees in that other place were not like those on earth. They stretched far too tall into that impossibly sky, and erratically throbbed with a pinkish-purple light.

Great trenches exposing rich soil and tree roots had been dug into the earth like small meteor blasts, at the ends of which lay massive, jagged chunks of the Wheel. I placed my hands on one of them. It was just plain old New Hampshire granite. Craggy, and covered with a lush skin of green moss, as if it had always been resting there.

I scrambled back to what had become the new top of the hill, and spun in a circle in an attempt to get my bearings. I'd been deposited in what seemed like a limitless expanse of those awful pulsating trees. The air smelled like lightning in a summer storm, and made my body hair stand on end as if I was grasping a static electricity globe at a science museum. An animalistic shriek sounded somewhere below me in the darkness of the wood, followed by a burst of what I first took to be spooked birds flying to safety, but then noticed their size; their too many wings, and the pink, glowing tendrils dangling behind them like clipped kite strings.

I sunk to my knees and started to cry. I was naked and disoriented in an unfathomable world with no obvious way of returning home to Claudia and the kids. The ground beneath me shook rhythmically, less like an earthquake and more like the footsteps of some impossibly large thing traversing the shadowy nightscape. The thrum of the boon I'd been so used to had ebbed away as I lay unconscious, leaving me feeling weak. Hollow. Aged.

Eventually I stood, and walked in a tight circle at the top of the shattered hill, scouring it with my eyes for a felled branch or even a small chunk of the Wheel that had enough of a jagged edge to do some damage. I was terrified and desperate to protect myself against whatever was in those woods because the eventuality of having to navigate them pressed on me. My left foot sunk into a soft patch of newly exposed dirt, sending me sprawling and screaming. I knew I'd sprained my ankle before I even hit the ground. The flash of pain bolted up my calf and hit my brain like a sock full of quarters.

Just as I was about to stand and attempt figuring out some way to brace my newly compromised leg, my eyes landed something; a patch of white in what looked like a natural clearing in the near distance. Was it just a random swath of flowering overgrowth? Or maybe a town? A cluster of children in white robes? And was that...was that faint singing I was hearing? I didn't know if it was real, or just my panicking brain injecting a droplet of hope into an otherwise hopeless situation.

As I picked my way back down the hill and started hiking in the general direction of what I prayed might be salvation, I thought about my odds. If I was lucky—the luckiest I'd have ever been in my life—I'd live out the rest of my years learning how to function in this impossible world as a sub-average, uncharmed man. My best-case scenario would be a life spent frustrating myself and my peers with the ineptitude I'd escaped as a child, and grieving the loss of a family I was almost relieved wouldn't have to witness me as I truly was. Would Claudia and Quinn and Dee-Dee grieve me in turn, or would the lapse of my boon shake them free from the shackles of the charmed aura that held my old life together, and find happiness without me; a happiness that was good and true.

Would I?

EPILOGUE

Dear Diary,

It's me, Quinn. I'm sorry it's been so long since I wrote something in here. The therapist says I should be writing stuff out as a way to process it, so here I am. This year has been...a lot. I don't even know where to begin.

I guess I should start with Dad stuff.

At first we just assumed Uncle Marley whisked him away on some insane vacation. Dubai. Ibiza. Mom said he used to do that all the time when we were still living in the city and too young to remember. She said he used to hate it, but it was the only way we could explain why he hadn't packed a bag or taken his phone, or even locked the doors. We were worried, but we weren't worried worried until those FBI agents came to the house asking us if we had any idea where everyone was.

They searched for months and months. They started with all the empty houses on the street, and then cut through Uncle Marley's fence and scoured the woodlands. When they found nothing, they increased their radius. The town. The state. The tri-state area. Before we really knew what was going on, there was a global manhunt for Dad, Uncle Marley, and Uncle Marley's parents. "MISSING BILLIONARE AND FAMILY KIDNAPPED FOR RANSOM?!" That's what was plastered all over the newspapers, but nobody ever called asking for money. News crews were parked at the top of the street for almost an entire year, and pounded on Mom's car whenever we needed to leave for school. It was pretty scary.

When the reporters and chaos became too much Mom eventually pulled us out of school entirely and paid for teachers come to the house. It was weird. I could barely pay attention. All I could think about was how guilty I felt, because for some reason I felt relieved and I couldn't understand why. I still don't understand now, but it was like a weight was lifted off my chest. Dee-Dee cried about Dad a lot back then, but eventually she told me she was mostly upset about how weirdly good she felt. Later, once Mom was done being drunk and sad, she said the same thing. So did Grammy and Popop when they came up from Florida to stay with us. My therapist calls it "trauma bonding."

I pretty much spent those months staring out through my bedroom window, hoping Dad would somehow stumble out of the woods full of stories and apologies and those big bear hugs he always gave me when he knew I needed them.

But he never did.

They declared Dad and Uncle Marley legally dead after only a year. Normally they wait a full seven before doing that. Mom said they probably did it because so many powerful people wanted to carve up Uncle Marley's billions for themselves, and that people like that—people like Uncle Marley—have a way of bending systems to suit their will. It probably didn't hurt that they hadn't found a trace of any of them. We held a funeral for Dad and Uncle Marley a week later, even though none of us believed they were actually dead. Empty caskets and everything. Dad's side of the church pews were filled with family and friends. Uncle Marley's side was almost empty, saved for a few people in fancy suits who spent the entire service looking at their phones and grumbling about their not being good cell service. They buried them together at the old cemetery down the street where Dad said he wanted to go when it was his time. Mom said we could visit it whenever we wanted, but I don't think I will.

Mom put our house on the market the next day and said we were moving back to the city. Apparently she'd called the library she worked at before she met Dad and somehow managed to get her old job back, no questions asked. None of us made a fuss, not even Dee-Dee who was pretty much the only one of us who actually liked it there. Angel came over to apologize for everything that happened between us as we were packing up the house. I hadn't seen her since we were pulled out of school, and didn't quite know what to say, so I just let her cry and hug me and say goodbye. I don't hate her or anything. I just hope she's happy one day.

I went over to Uncle Marley's house to make myself one more ice cream before we left, but don't tell Mom. She'd be so pissed. We've been back in New York for three years now. It's weird how good it feels to be here after having spent so much time nestled in the woods, away from everything and everyone. I expected the perpetual car alarms and loud talking and overflowing dumpsters and homeless people to be jarring, but I haven't slept this well in...I couldn't tell you how long. And Dee-Dee is straight-up thriving. She's killing it in third grade and at sports, and she's an absolute virtuoso on a violin. Mom says it's because we grew up with all the sounds and smells and sights of the city as babies so it's nurturing for us, but that doesn't feel quite right because Mom feels good too and she didn't grow up here. It's more than that. It's more than the white noise outside the windows of our little apartment, and it's more than reconnecting with my old friends from before we moved away. Sometimes when I'm in therapy I feel like I'm getting close to putting a finger on what it is, but then it sifts between my fingers like beach sand. Maybe I'll never figure out why we've been so happy since Dad went missing. Maybe I don't need to. Gifts and horses and mouths, and all that stuff.

I guess that's enough for now, Diary. Thanks for letting me talk, er, write, or whatever. I promise I won't be a stranger. And hey, if you happen to see Dad, tell him I love him and that we're doing great, will you? Tell him we're not mad. Tell him we miss him, because we do. We really do.

~ Quinn

BONUS STORY: LORD OF DOORS

Andy and Jenna sat around a patio stone fire pit in Pete and Kayla's backyard, waiting for the mushrooms to kick in as the evening sun gave way to a peach sherbet sunset.

Andy knew it had been a rough month for Jenna after losing her job as a commercial artist. The marketing firm she'd been with for nearly a decade culled most of her department in favor of generative AI software, and she'd had no luck finding employment since. That was why Pete and Kayla insisted on hosting Jenna's birthday party at their freshly renovated home.

The mushrooms had been Pete's idea. "All of our kids are with babysitters for the night. Let's fucking cut loose. When's the last time we had fun? Like, real fun?"

Pete's little baggie full of psychedelics prompted plenty of *absolutely nots* and *what's wrong with yous*, after which the four of them swiftly agreed, and washed the mushrooms down with their respective cans of beer and glasses of wine.

Andy and Pete talked about the differences between their health insurance plans. Kayla and Jenna giggled about the expired mail-in DNA tests Andy ordered for them a while back.

"I got the results email last week. It said you were my granddaughter. Like, great granddaughter times five, or something!"

The two women howled with laughter. Kayla came over and wrapped Jenna in a big hug. "I love you so much, Nanna!"

"You're so grown up! I remember when you were just knee-high to a grasshopper!" Jenna said.

"Andy's so cheap he's buying DNA kits out of the clearance bin!"

Andy chuckled, and walked inside to grab a fresh beer, the telltale euphoric body sensations that come with a psilocybin experience beginning to kick into high gear, and stopped to regard a painting on the wall in the dining room. He hadn't paid it much attention during the meal as his back had been facing it, but with a head full of psilocybin and booze, he was suddenly captivated by the strangeness of it.

The old oil painting, its surface veined in thin craquelure that communicated its great age, didn't remotely fit the modern new décor of the renovated room. The peeling black lacquer of its antique wooden frame contrasted abominably against the freshly painted wall behind it. Three Yankee fishermen toiling away on a rocky New Hampshire shoreline at twilight were depicted in chunky oil strokes. The sky above them was a roiling mass of gunmetal storm clouds, the ocean black as burned oil, save for the whitecaps of waves.

"Ah, I see you've discovered this grotesque piece of shit!" Pete wandered in. He was carrying a handful of beers back out to the fire pit when he noticed the transfixed Andy in the dining room.

"Where did you get it? I can't stop staring at it."

"Oh man, you're gonna love this story. Kayla's great-great-great-great-grandmother Judith Bezanson was some kind of artist, and demanded this thing get handed down from mother to daughter on her death bed. They've been doing that for a little over two hundred years. What is that, six? Seven generations?"

Andy marveled at Pete's backstory, running a finger along the crackling lacquer of the frame as he listened.

"Of course, Kayla's mom demanded we inherit this creepy thing the second we finished remodeling, and it's not like we could say no, right? No way we're gonna be the ones to break that streak. Now I get to stare at it as I eat my morning cereal for the rest of my life. Jesus, it looks even creepier on mushrooms."

With that, Pete vacated the dining room, leaving Andy to watch as the details of the painting pulsed and swirled in his hallucinogenic haze. Through a window, laughter and the crackle of damp wood being thrown onto the fire reminded him he should rejoin the party.

Just as he was turning to leave, Andy caught a flash of movement in the corner of his eye. Maybe it was a flicker of an overhead light as the electrical grid strained under the heft of ten-thousand cranked air conditioners. Maybe a stray moth fluttering near a bulb. He turned back to the painting. He allowed his eyes to unfocus, giving him a wider range of vision with which to catch whatever it was.

His eyes reflexively snapped back into focus, landing on one of the fishermen in the painting who was suddenly no longer frozen in a prison of desiccated pigment. Ocean spray beaded on his grey beard and oiled wool jacket as he strained to drag a heavy net onto the beach. Andy's mouth opened and closed like a freshly caught haddock as he watched black waves break on an inhospitable shore.

"OK, I'm tripping my balls off", he announced to the empty room before settling down at the table to let the old painting melt and twist for his amusement. "This is fucking great."

The three weather-hardened fishermen toiled away, hurrying to load their meager catch of cod into the fishery, and secure their gear with lengths of hemp rope before the storm blew all the way in. A canvas tarp tied over the skeletal wooden frame of a partially built schooner lashed erratically in the stiff wind. Andy knew if audible hallucinations ever decided to join the visual feast, he'd hear that tarp snap and crack in the air like a lion tamer's bullwhip.

The fisherman with the grey beard, someone Andy was beginning to think held seniority over the other two, yelled silent orders into the driving rain. There was a manic frenzy in their eyes. Andy had known men with eyes like that before. They were the eyes of men who were just barely surviving the grueling lives handed down to them.

"What are you doing in here, Silly Billy?"

Andy's gaze was wrenched away from the show playing out within the boundaries of the lacquered frame by Jenna. In her hands was a plastic action figure; some kind of futuristic space soldier from the playroom past the kitchen. The green of her eyes was almost completely eclipsed by her dilated pupils.

"I can't stop staring at this painting. It's crazy. Everything is moving!"

"Oh yeah, look at that. It's all melty and swirly. That's fun! This was a great idea. I'm so glad we're enjoying ourselves."

"Can you see the fishermen, like, moving around and stuff?"

Jenna squinted, and leaned over the table to get a better look.

"No, it's all just regular melty and swirly, like everything else. Are you coming outside? You have to look at the trees. The trees are *so weird.*"

"I'll be out in a second", Andy lied. Contented with his answer, Jenna walked away.

The perimeter of the fenced-in yard was marked with flickering citronella tiki torches. Loud Top-40 hits from the 90s blasted from a speaker lost somewhere in the grass. Kayla, was seated next to the small fire pit, which Pete was feeding more split wood into. Andy launched into excited detail about what he'd been seeing in the painting, but Jenna only half paid attention as she lay on her stomach in the grass, and studiously arranging a small pile of action figures from Pete and Kayla's children's room into various poses.

"What are you up to, babe?" Andy asked Jenna. "Having fun?"

"I'm recreating a panel from Bosch's *The Last Judgment* triptych!"

"Very cool and normal!" Andy said. He hadn't been in the yard for five minutes, and he was already feeling compelled to go back inside to stare at the painting. "I'm gonna grab a beer inside. You need anything?"

"I'm good!" Jenna said, never prying her eyes from her work. "Maybe get me some more action figures?"

By the time Andy got back to the dining room, the scene in the painting had changed.

The clouds had burned off, giving way to a bruised, sunsetting sky over the Atlantic. Andy cracked a beer and watched as the three fishermen stood around what looked like some kind of yellowish boulder laying on the beach. The rope net lying next to it gave Andy the impression that they'd accidentally scooped it up from the ocean floor, and from the look of their stooped, hands-on-hips postures, they didn't know what to make of it.

Red Pants said something to Grey Beard which Andy couldn't make out. Grey Beard seemed to repeat back what Red Pants said, but that time Andy was able to read Grey Beard's wind-chapped lips.

Wax. Candlewax.

And

Smells like flowers. Expensive candlewax.

The three men began scraping away big globs of fragrant wax, making sure to deposit them in a rickety wooden Wheelbarrow for future use. Andy drained his beer as he watched, and went to get a fresh one. When he sat back down, Grey Beard, Red Pants, and Other Guy, the third fisherman, were marveling at an elaborately carved wooden trunk. Its heavy lid and body were adorned with an intricate golden inlay pattern that spoke of masterful craftsmanship. An ornate padlock was strung through thick iron loops in front. It certainly wasn't the trunk of an impoverished New Englander; more like that of a wealthy shipping magnate, or a highly decorated military officer.

Other Guy spoke, and the other two nodded in agreement: *Pirates.*

That made sense to Andy. A big, fancy trunk encased in wax to waterproof it before sinking it to the ocean floor? That was a pirate move if he'd ever heard of one, and he knew from school the New England coast had a long, rich history of piracy. It had probably been stashed there by some enterprising smuggler to be retrieved at a later date once the heat was off him.

"Fucking open it already!" Andy was on the edge of his seat, riveted by the discovery. "I bet it's full of gold doubloons or some shit!"

As if the characters in the painting could hear Andy's demands,

Red Pants picked up a softball-sized rock from the beach, smooth from eons of contact with the tides, and approached the trunk lid. Several well-delivered bashes later, the padlock fell to the sand with what Andy imagined was a loud clatter.

Grey Beard shoved Red Pants aside, and opened the trunk lid. The three fishermen peered inside, silently taking inventory of the contents.

"What's in it? What's in it?!" Andy was standing up, yelling at the painting as if it were a baseball game on TV.

Other Guy reached inside, and pulled out a large leather-bound book. His leathery face drooped with disappointment.

Books. It's nothing but blasted books in here.

Grey Beard reached inside next, emerging with two armfuls of ancient looking volumes. He set some down on the sand, freeing up a hand to examine one more closely. He flipped through browned pages filled with texts and diagrams Andy couldn't make out.

Old. Rarified. These'll fetch a handsome price at market. Richies love stuffing their libraries with books like these.

"ANDY, GET THE FUCK BACK OUT HERE!"

Pete bellowed at Andy from the backyard, after which Kayla, and Jenna howled with laughter.

By 2:00 am, Jenna's birthday party was still going strong. Fearing the effects were beginning to wane, they'd all eaten more mushrooms around midnight, and were beaming harder than ever. Andy had tried getting them to watch the painting with him, but nobody was able to see what he was seeing, so they contented themselves by wandering around the house, arguing with bathroom doors, and reaching revelations about their legs each having their own individual personalities.

For a time, Andy was content to join the rest of the group in their psychedelic exploration of the remodeled house. He was tripping just as hard as they were, and enjoyed discovering new things that looked out of proportion to their sensory distorted eyes.

But through it all, he couldn't stop thinking about the painting.

Eventually, deciding his wife and friends were sufficiently preoccupied, Andy slipped away, reclaiming his seat at the dining room table.

Night had once again descended on the painted shoreline. The fishermen had built a driftwood bonfire, and were seated on around it on apple crates. They laughed as they filled their tin mugs from an unlabeled bottle, and sang shanties Andy wished to hell he could hear.

"Oh good, you guys are partying too." Andy raised his beer in a toast, and took a long pull. "Celebrating your big windfall. Hell yeah."

Grey Beard stood up, and stumbled backwards a bit before regaining his equilibrium. The old man clearly couldn't hold his liquor like Red Pants and Other Guy, who guffawed as their boss stumbled over to the open trunk, and pulled out a random book. He danced around the campfire with it, spurring the other two into cackling fits. Grey Beard drunkenly leafed through pages, only stopping to leer at the unfamiliar diagrams and symbols Andy could now see because the old fisherman was standing closer to the painting's point of reference.

Grey Beard grabbed a stick, and inelegantly recreated one of the symbols in the wet sand; a crude glyph that looked like a head with two faces trapped within a triangle within a circle.

At that, Red Pants stood up and shouted. *Witchcraft! I knows witchcraft when I sees it!*

They hooted and hollered. Grey Beard offered the strange book to Red Pants, who held up his hands, and shook his head vehemently. Other Guy snatched it from Grey Beard, and, after rifling through several pages, began to read some passages from it. Andy couldn't understand most of the words Other Guy was theatrically bellowing into the night air, but he was able to pick up on some.

[Unintelligible] The shunned deity known as Akkakus [unintelligible] Gibbering Saints [unintelligible] the closest any world religion has come to [unintelligible] the Roman god Janus [unintelligible] representatives of beginnings and endings, frames, Lord of Doors, Akkakus [unintelligible] two-headed [unintelligible] has taken refuge in Ether's Wood, the unmapped interspatial "waystation" which was previously the domain of [unintelligible]. A group of experts heretofore referred to as The Explorers of Ether's Wood has been assembled to chart this territory [unintelligible]

Andy laughed along with the fishermen. "Wow, OK. Those books are *weird* weird."

Other Guy flipped through a few more pages, and then pointed an excited finger when he landed on something of note.

The Akkakus Incantation!

Grey Beard laughed so hard he started coughing. Red Pants bolted up and waved his hands, the lone superstitious member of the trio, unwilling to toy with even the most absurd supernatural goofery. Grey Beard dismissed him, and insisted Other Guy continue.

"Don't be a buzzkill, Red Pants! Let's hear it, Other Guy! Give us the double-double-toil-and-trouble!" Andy yelled at the painting.

Red Pants filled his mug to overflowing, and took a soul-fortifying swig from it. Other Guy moved closer to the fire so he'd have light to read by, and proceeded to orate a string of curious words Andy couldn't bring himself to understand, regardless of how much he concentrated on Other Guy's silently moving mouth.

Grey Beard stopped laughing, and became enraptured by whatever Other Guy was reading. Red Pants moved behind an outcropping of jagged rocks to take a piss. Other Guy continued rattling off the unintelligible incantation of Akkakus for his audience, absent-mindedly wandering on the beach until he'd found himself standing in the center of the two-headed glyph Grey Beard had carved into the damp sand moments earlier.

The scene within the frame suddenly shuddered. Andy dropped his beer on the floor and brought his hands to his stinging eyes. His half-digested dinner threatened to see the light of day for the second time, but he wrestled his gorge down, and brought his eyes back to the painting.

There, maybe ten feet away from the bonfire on the beach, rested a white two-door 1993 Eagle Talon. Andy was immediately sure of the year, make, and model, as he'd driven a nearly identical coupe in high school.

"What...the fuck..."

The three fishermen stood around the futuristic carriage made of metal and plastic, gawking at it as if it were some kind of crash-landed alien spaceship, and rightly so. The first automobile prototype probably wasn't due to debut for another eighty years or so, and it would be another hundred before that particular one began rolling off the assembly line.

Grey Beard poked it with a stick, and instantly recoiled. Other Guy had dropped the book, and sobbed uncontrollably. Red Pants clutched his head and screamed about having accidentally opened a doorway to hell with that damned book.

The devil's very chariot, I tell you!

Andy let out a snort. It might not have been Satan's hot rod, but he'd certainly had a devilishly good time in that backseat after his senior prom.

After some wildly impassioned debate between the three drunken fishermen, Grey Beard brought everyone to a silence so he could speak.

Whatever this thing is, it'll sell for a small fortune. The book did this, somehow. Those words.

Wide-eyed, the men regarded each other.

Grey Beard barked an order to Other Guy. *Do it again.*

Red Pants instantly protested. *We're meddling with demonic witchery! Look at this- this thing -you've summoned! We mustn't! We should burn these books! Send them back to hell where they belong!*

Red Pants grabbed a flaming piece of driftwood from the bonfire, and rushed toward the open trunk on the beach.

"Oh fuck!" Andy said, leaning forward to take in the action.

Grey Beard reached into his pocket, retrieving a small revolver, and aimed it at Red Pants. Andy never heard the pop of the revolver, but he watched as Red Pants' body went stiff, and keeled over onto the beach, the burning log resting on his bare neck. His arms and legs spasmed, and then finally went still.

Other Guy dropped the book on the beach, and backed up slowly, his hands up in a gesture of surrender.

Do it again, Grey Beard said. Other Guy sputtered something unintelligible Andy couldn't quite catch, but believed it to be a terrified refusal.

A second gout of smoke exited the revolver's barrel. The top of

Other Guy's skull exploded in a pink mist that was instantly carried away on the ocean breeze. His body hit the beach like a stone.

Grey Beard tucked his gun away, and stood in the center of the symbol. He picked the book up from the beach and briefly turned to the ocean, noting how close the tide was coming to erasing the strange conjuring glyph, and hurriedly flipped through the pages until he found the one with the incantation on it.

Andy watched with a mixture of revulsion and curiosity as the murderous Grey Beard attempted to give life to the alien words on the page.

[Unintelligible] *Akkakus* [unintelligible] *señor de las puertas* [unintelligible] *saints baragouins* [unintelligible] *lemnul eterului vi ber deg om det profer ostium* [unintelligible]

The painting shivered again. Andy felt his gorge rise. When he looked again, the car had disappeared from the beach. Astonished, Grey Beard repeated the words as the edge of the frothy tide began lapping at Other Guy's corpse.

Sit laus to Akkakus [unintelligible] *señor de las puertas fugiendum unum saints baragouins* [unintelligible] *lemnul eterului* [unintelligible] *doa o akeru* [unintelligible]

Andy ran into the kitchen and vomited foamy beer into the sink. When he returned, Grey Beard was staring up at a modern three-story printing press. Andy only recognized what it was because of a documentary about the newspaper industry he'd fallen asleep to several months earlier. Its steel I-beam skeleton stuffed with rollers and belts and wires and buttons loomed over the terrified old fisherman, who immediately turned back to the book, and rattled off the incantation as best he could. Seeing it coming, Andy preemptively looked away from the painting before it could make him sick again.

For the next half hour, Andy watched with rapt attention as the murderous Grey Beard experimented with the incantation, becoming more fluid with the pronunciations as he went. Waves crashed over the bodies of Other Guy and Red Pants as strange things appeared and disappeared on the beach with every pass. An early 2000s flip phone. A bag of pasta. An electric guitar with the neck snapped in half. A giant redwood that climbed so high into the night sky the painting's frame couldn't begin to accommodate it. A black sea slug the size of a small dog. A lacy pink bra, which Grey Beard examined with a level of enraptured interest only found in lonely men who haven't known the touch of a woman in some time. An avocado green electric typewriter. A pile of corpses awaiting burial from a Civil War battlefield.

Sit laus to Akkakus [unintelligible] *señor de las puertas fugiendum unum saints baragouins* [unintelligible] *lemnul eterului vi ber deg om det profer ostium doa o akeru* [unintelligible]

That time, the painting didn't shake. Instead, a crack of lightning illuminated the vast expanse of the night-blackened coast. In that split second, Andy got the briefest impression of a being standing on the rocky shore. It was monstrously tall, its too-large head featuring a pair of grimacing human faces pointing in different directions. It filled Andy with a sense of revulsion, and, was it also reverence? The entity's too-long arm, ending in a gnarled, blackened finger the length of a harpoon, pointed toward the last living fisherman on that beach; a gesture that reminded Andy of his father. A scolding, wordless act meant to instantly curb a child's bad behavior. And then, it was gone.

"Hey Andy!" It was Kayla from upstairs. "Is Jenna down there with you?"

Andy, still dazzled by the increasingly wild events taking place in the painting, shook himself into the present.

"No! She's not up there with you?"

Kayla and Pete clomped down the stairs in a tight line, each looking mildly concerned.

"Well she's not upstairs. We just checked every room."

"I can tell you she's certainly not *downstairs*", Andy said. "The stairs are right behind me. I would've have known."

Pete stormed through the kitchen and out into the backyard, shouting Jenna's name. Kayla, beginning to doubt herself, ran back upstairs to double-check each room.

"Has anyone tried her phone?" Andy said, reaching for his. "I'm sure she's goofing around with her little action figures somewhere."

Andy found Jenna's name in his recent call list, and clicked on it.

Hi, you've reached Jenna. Leave a message at the beep!

"What the fuck?" Andy said as he hung up, and tried again, this time putting it on speakerphone.

Hi, you've reached Jenna. Leave a message at the beep!

"What's happening?" Kayla said and she rushed back down the stairs empty handed. "What's going on?"

Kayla and Pete's house became a frenzy of activity. After scouring the entire neighborhood with flashlights in the wee hours of the morning, they decided to call the police. Nosy neighbors peered out of windows and stepped onto their front porches in their bathrobes to watch as two cruisers pulled up to the house around 5:00 am.

One by one, the partygoers were made to detail the night's events for an officer seated at the dining room table, who took notes on a small pad of paper. Everyone admitted to having partied a little too hard, a fact the officers had no doubt of considering the state of the house, and the size of everyone's dinner plate pupils.

When it was Andy's turn to offer a statement, he plonked down at the table, and nervously glanced at the painting behind the officer's head. Once again, the scene had changed, and Andy's face mutated into a mask of unbridled panic.

A pale woman knelt on the beach, shaking and holding herself by the light of the bonfire that still burned there. Her clothing, partially obscured by the flickering of the firelight, looked clean, but ragged, as if they'd been dragged behind a car on the freeway for several miles. Her hair hung in front of her face. Grey Beard stood over the cowering woman, his eyes wide with his pleasure and good fortune.

"It can't be." Andy said, prompting the officer to lay his pen down, and reassess the hallucinating man in front of him. "It fucking can't be."

"Sir?"

Grey Beard scooped her up over his shoulder in a fireman's carry, her small fists beating the meat of his broad back until both of them disappeared from the field of view.

"She's in the fucking painting! Jenna is in the fucking painting! We have to get her out!"

Andy lunged for the painting on the wall, and the officer restrained him. Shortly after that, he was sedated, strapped on an EMT's gurney, and headed to the local hospital for a detox hold.

Rain cascaded down the windows of Andy's grimy one-bedroom apartment, the soundtrack to his depressive state the buzzing of flies over a sink full of old dishes. A wall matted with yellowing newspaper clippings reading HUNT FOR MISSING WOMAN GROWS COLD and HUBBY DETAINED ON SUSPICION OF DISAPPEARING HIS WIFE loomed like an accusatory storm cloud. Andy sat on the floor in nothing but a pair of three-day-old boxers, his back against a stained futon couch, and stared.

The cracked old painting was propped up from the mildewing carpet on a pair of red milk crates, and leaned against the wall opposite the futon. He'd used the last of his last savings buying it from Kayla and Pete, who wanted nothing to do with the old familial obligation after Jenna vanished. Andy swigged from a plastic jug, the warm, astringent vodka filling his brain and body with a grief-dulling sickness.

He'd tried everything to get the painting to come to life again. Day after heartbreaking day, Andy would eat handfuls of mushrooms and wait for Grey Beard, Red Pants, and Other Guy to become unstuck in time; to give him some kind of clue as to how he could pry his wife out of that dark beach, and back into his arms.

When mushrooms proved ineffective, he tried other drugs. Acid, ecstasy, painkillers. In an act of desperation, he once bought a bag of heroin-"to snort, not shoot", he told the dealer who couldn't have cared less—but all it did was make him vomit for hours on end.

"Why won't you work? Why won't you fucking work?" Andy mumbled his frustrated mantra, his volume ranging from quiet, choking sobs, to enraged bellowing that set neighbors to pounding on shared walls.

With the dregs of the vodka bottle emptied, a slow rage began building in Andy, as it often did. He lunged for the painting, grabbed it by its frame, and slammed it down on the floor, forcing the corner of one of the milk crates through the canvas, and out the other side.

Realizing what he'd done, Andy grabbed fistfuls of his hair and screamed, earning himself another volley of thumping and complaining from the neighbors. He gasped like a beached mackerel as he glared at the hole he'd put in the painting. His only chance to make things right. He'd ruined it.

He sunk to his knees, and examined the torn brown paper backing of the painting with a trembling hand. It felt crumbly to the touch along the edges of the newly tattered flaps.

Andy was about to look for a roll of scotch tape when his eyes landed on something underneath the ripped backing. He reached in, and retrieved what appeared to be a small bundle of folded papers secured by a small length of twine.

Stunned by the discovery, Andy shuffled back to the futon and sat, pulling on one end of the twine until the bow came undone.

He unfolded a newspaper clipping that was so old it felt like he was holding a sheet of onion skin in his hands. It was from the January 1841 edition of the New Hampshire Gazette, the state's oldest running newspaper. Andy glanced over the archaic words on the page. A man making a formal announcement that his son was taking over the family business, and that he wouldn't claim any of his profits, nor pay any of his debts from that moment forward. A death notice for a woman who'd been struck down by a runaway carriage. A man was once again placed into custody for being "drunk on rum and pulling up his neighbor's turnips."

Then, Andy froze.

BEZANSON ESCAPES THE NOOSE -- Judith Bezanson, renowned local artist and wife of ground fishery operator Morgan Bezanson, was found mentally unfit during her murder trial. She will spend her remaining days in the New Hampshire Asylum for the Insane.

Andy bolted up from the futon, and pulled the broken painting off the floor. He looked at the dory on the black beach. BEZANSON FISHERY.

Andy feverishly shuffled through the bundle of ancient papers, scouring them for more information. A well-preserved daguerreotype slid from between the quill-written fishery profit sheets and court documentation, and landed at his feet.

Depicted in frozen sepia was a stern-faced woman. She was posed in a wooden chair, and dressed in hospital linens designed to offer a sense of uniformity among an incarcerated population. Her fading blonde hair was tied back in a severe bun. Her eyes glared back at Andy through the years, and conveyed a single, unmistakable message to him. *This is what became of me.*

Her hands, positioned in her lap, clutched a futuristic space soldier plastic action figure.

ACKNOWLEDGMENTS

You've made it to the end! Now you get to watch your humble author stammer and flail as he writes his very first acknowledgement section. How does one even do this? Let's find out together.

I'd like to start by thanking the people who were instrumental in making this project a reality. Kristy Baptist, Steve Wands, Anna Kubik, and Megan Yundt at Dead Sky Publishing are all incredible folks who understood my vision for *Feeding the Wheel,* and helped me turn it into something I truly love. Alex Woodroe, my developmental editor and consigliere, is next on the list for not calling the cops when I first shared a story idea from my notes app that read something like "giant stone wheel that spits a rooster tail of gore into the sky as children with clasped hands sing." Chris Krawczyk from Little Ghost Books and Charles Tyra from Cosmic Horror Monthly get a window-shattering thunderclap of a high five for giving my earliest stories a chance, and injecting me with the confidence I needed for longer works. My superstar wife Jessica gets my heart (and the rest of my organs) for continuing to believe in me as I attempt the impossible over and over again.

There's simply not enough room to include everyone who deserves praise and recognition for the roles they've played in putting this book in your hands, but I do want to take a moment to thank you; the reader. Your money is hard-earned, and you chose to gamble some of it on an author you've most likely never heard of before. That means a whole hell of a lot to me, and I won't soon forget it.

Finally, I'd like to thank the state of New Hampshire for allowing me to spend my fleeting life in its grand and terrifying embrace. There has never been a more potent well of inspiration, nor a more solacing slice of the world to call home. This is for you.

ABOUT THE AUTHOR

Michael Boulerice (he/him) is a lifelong resident of New Hampshire who spends his winters snowboarding in the White Mountains, and his summers lounging by the coast. When he's not doing that, he's writing, acting as Mr. FixIt for a span of businesses and properties, tinkering on his ancient Volkswagen, and being held hostage by his two spoiled cats Charlie and Sydney. He's had stories published in magazines like *Cosmic Horror Monthly* and *Thank You For Joining the Algorithm*, anthologies like *Monster Lairs* and *Your Flight Has Been Cancelled*, and have been adapted for audio by venues like *NoSleep* and *The Creepy Podcast*. For more information about Michael's works and whereabouts, please visit michaelboulerice.com.

ALSO BY MICHAEL BOULERICE

In Pursuit of the Black Chuck Wagon: Monster Lairs / Dark Matter Ink

Your Posh Revelries Will Be Claimed by My Currents: Cosmic Horror Monthly #47

Nose Beers: The NoSleep Podcast